Praise for *Gloss*

'Taut and vivid. It is like ste
described hallucinatory nigh
mesmerised all the way through. The themes of coercive control and psychological disintegration are so chilling and important.'
– Suzanne Joinson, author of *The Museum of Lost and Fragile Things*

Praise for *Little Bandaged Days*

'Gripping, composed, observant, wonderfully written and extravagantly cruel.'
— Daisy Hildyard, *Guardian*

'Beautifully written and frighteningly honest.'
— Eithne Farry, Sunday *Express*

'Wilder artfully cranks up the tension, so you don't quite know when you begin to hold your breath. A chilling read.'
— Oyinkan Braithwaite, author of *My Sister, the Serial Killer*

By the same author
Little Bandaged Days

GLOSS

Kyra Wilder

LesFugitives

London

This first English-language edition published
by Les Fugitives editions in the United Kingdom in 2025 •
• Les Fugitives Ltd, 91 Cholmley Gardens, Fortune Green Road, London NW6 1UN •
• www.lesfugitives.com • Cover design by Sarah Schulte •
• Text design by Juliette Lépineau • All rights reserved •
• No part of this publication may be reproduced, stored in a retrieval
system or transmitted in any form or by any means, electronic,
mechanical, photocopying, recording or otherwise, without
prior permission in writing from Les Fugitives editions •
• A CIP catalogue record for this book is available from the British Library •
• The rights of Kyra Wilder to be identified as author of this
work have been identified in accordance with Section 77 of the
Copyright, Designs and Patents Act 1988 •
• Printed by Petro ofsetas • ISBN: 978-1-7397783-5-4 •

the quick brown fox

'You do not have to be good.'
— Mary Oliver

Girls' Choir

in the garden

There was one day where we took a drive in Lee's van, piling all in the back. We were all the same knees and elbows, like one of us had six instead of only two apiece. We were close with each other then like that.

Then we didn't have anywhere to go so Lee just drove us, out through the stubble-grass hills tangled up like sisters and quiet like little girls. We looked out the window, watching each other, watching nothing much. The days were washing over us and making us better and cleaning us out and we could let them. We could let the days do that.

Lee said that we were doing well and praised us. And when he praised us, we could let ourselves do that thing where we came a bit alive and snuggled and got close to one another in the back of the van. Because it was only us and Lee and all those golden apples growing at the farm and there was no one else to look.

When we came to his house, to his garden, hidden in the dip between two hills, Lee told us to be relieved. You're home, he told us. This place is meant for you. He said that we should hang our outside selves up beside the door like out-of-season coats. He was right and we were so relieved. Relieved not to be anything. To be sloughed off. Not being anything there in his garden, being nothing, we could eat.

Driving slowly down a wooded road, we saw a great blue heron walking in the grass. We stopped to watch him because we had the time. Lee turned off the engine and we leaned back in our seats and chewed our nails, right down and red just like we liked to, until Lee told us all to stop.

And we did stop but we left our fingers in our mouths, barely breathing, just watching it, the big old lumpy bird, the way it walked.

Suddenly the heron snapped his head into the grass and came back up with a thick black snake scissored in his beak. He rocked back and forth and we watched breathless, while the ragged heron began to squeeze the life out of the snake. We sat unmoving, frozen behind the dirty windows of Lee's van until the snake hung heavy, slumped in the bird's beak.

Now it moved so slowly. Not as if it were in pain, but as if it had forgotten only just that quickly how to be alive. It's just giving up! we said, biting each other's fingers and sucking in our cheeks. The bird's beak bore deep into the muscled body of the snake, almost splitting it in two yet still, the snake just hung there. We wondered if maybe it was dead.

Suddenly, the snake rolled over, tearing its skin on the heron's jaw and we grinned and thought that maybe there would be a fight. We pinched the insides of each other's arms and thought of it, the way the snake might wrench itself free. And we licked our lips and thought too of the damage it might do to its own self trying to escape. But we were disappointed, the snake only flipped itself over so it could better slip its tail down the side of the bird's neck. And we gasped when we saw how it was almost a caress. Then the bird threw back its head and gulped the snake down clumsily. And then it was suddenly so intimate between them that we thought maybe we should look away.

We didn't though. We couldn't. We kept our eyes on the two of them together and we flicked our own tongues against our lips. It was only as the last bit of the snake was swallowed that it began to fight. We watched the bird lose its balance as the snake inside it thrashed and we squeezed each other's hands and thought maybe the snake could still somehow get out. After an awful moment though, there was only stillness and the blue heron hefted itself up heavily into the air.

We sat inert, beside ourselves, horrified and utterly bereft until Lee pushed back from the steering wheel and laughed. And then we wondered if he'd known before about the bird, if the bird had been the point. And we snapped to attention, trying to recall the details just exactly, thinking this might be a lesson or a test. We reached for each other down beneath the seats where Lee couldn't see us and we wished that we were back at the farm where we were safe.

Before coming to Lee's farm, we had tried to bring our bodies back to life by means of our own invention. By starving them, by cutting them, by digging into them and carving them out. Then we had come to Golden Apples and we had tried to listen to Lee because if we did what he told us, if we polished the apples and if we tended the trees, he said that we would live. And we had lived. But we wondered, craning our necks to see the disappearing heron, when had the snake been dead? It seemed colossally important that we should know.

When had it been too late for it to save itself? From the beginning? From the moment the bird snapped his head into the grass? We wondered if that had been why Lee had brought us. To see how it didn't matter if the snake wriggled, if it tried, or if it didn't try, to escape. Underneath the seats, we braided our fingers anxiously together. Lee, Eleni said, let's please go back.

PART I

(girls like me are liars)

four months before the trial

Eleni

There was a right moment to slip across the dance floor. The crowd moved like water does, like they all do, all the slightly drunk crowds at weddings. Pulling together, coming apart, waves and trickles and feet, dancing just off-beat and smiling. There was always a right moment to cut through with my silver tray of drinks. I just had to watch for an opening, a break in the crush of bodies that was the size and shape of me.

I could have walked around the dance floor. I could have offered drinks only at the edges, but I liked to go right through the middle of the crowd. I liked it because I wanted them to touch me, the dancers, the guests. I always wanted them to touch me, and they would. They especially would at the end of the night. When they were loose and uncareful with their bodies. The back of a hand would brush my arm, a hip would briefly push against my hip. I loved it. The shiver of the dresses, the men with their top buttons undone, their suit vests open, all the flapping fabric sometimes wisping lightly up against my skin. The way they jostled me and sloshed the drinks. The way they moved me like they moved for just a moment. As if I were a part of it, that wild, reckless swell. I loved the scritch of their beads, their jewelry, their bracelets and their rings, the way they snagged sometimes on my black server's vest. It was irresistible, the way they sometimes caught me for a moment by a thread.

Sometimes a hand would reach out and touch me, my eyebrow maybe or the side of my face. Or sometimes fingers would brush against my ribs reaching for a drink.

As if they knew me, those fingers, or as if they didn't know me and it didn't matter. I would lean into it, that hand, just a little. Not doing anything really that I had to admit to, but leaning slightly anyway, pressing even into it with my tray of drinks. I liked those nights, those parties, when it was late, when the whole crowd was pushing in on me. The weight of it, the heat, the obliterating crush.

Tasks were like that too, like crowds, if there were enough of them. They kept you grounded, but in a place outside yourself. Anyone could fill a hundred cups with ice or polish a thousand champagne flutes and while I did it, I could be anyone too.

I wanted to be useful all the time. I wanted to move from one task to the next without ever stopping. I said as much to Mitch when he interviewed me for the job and it had made him laugh, but I'd said that I was serious. That I really loved folding napkins and stacking plates. After that, he'd mostly just wanted to know if I could work on short notice, any day of the week. My schedule was wide open, I'd said.

I'd found Mitch when I'd come to look at a room I'd seen advertised on Craigslist. Cheap, private, available immediately, the ad had said, which pretty much checked all the boxes. But still, you don't want to go in showing that. That you don't care about the details. That you don't mind. You've got to keep that sort of thing to yourself.

Mitch's place was a big house on Cedar, six bedrooms spread out over two floors, plus apartments in the basement and the attic. Mitch said it belonged to his aunt. He had recently dropped out of culinary school, though that wasn't how he'd put it, and his aunt let him live in the house for free, as long as he found tenants and collected rent.

When I'd gone to see about the room, Mitch had

answered the door holding a sloshing plastic bag full of what turned out to be fish heads. Got these for free, he'd said, his dry lips working around an unlit cigarette. Those fucks at Berkeley Bowl throw them out. Can you believe it? I'm going to make the most amazing fumet you ever tasted here in a minute, he'd said, pulling me in like we already knew each other. Grabbing me a little hard, like somehow, he could tell. Like he already knew that he could.

Inside, there was the smell of leeks melting in butter. Honestly, he said, heading back into the kitchen, talking almost only to himself, it's going to blow your mind.

I followed him through to the kitchen where a pot was just coming to a simmer on the stove. He slit open the bag, dumped it in the sink and plucked a head out of the slimy pink ice. You're here for the room, right? he said, sliding tattooed fingers up inside the head and snapping off the gills. Just a minute and I'll show it to you, he told me, moving through the heads methodically, pulling out the gills and flicking them into the trash.

The room turned out to be only really a walk-in closet off the first-floor landing. It had a high ceiling though and blue walls and a stained-glass window that cut the light up into pieces – made it soft and broken-up and just right. There was a bed with a little table next to it and a lamp. My room's up there, Mitch said, pointing up to the attic. You can slip the rent under my door the first of the month.

He asked me what I did for work and I told him I was between jobs. I had been working on a farm, I told him, out near Marin. Picking apples, I said. Oh shit, Mitch said, the produce out there is unbelievable. I said, yeah, but it hadn't worked out. I told him I was ready for something else.

He asked me how long I had been out there, and I told him I had been there quite a while and he said that he could get me work. Catering, he said. Dinner parties. Weddings. All you'd have to do is smile and hold trays of drinks. I'll tell them that you're in the industry, he told me. Considering the farming, he said. You'll make rent easy, just off tips.

We drove all over the East Bay catering. Sometimes into the city and sometimes up into the hills for private events. Mitch would cook and I would hold napkins and pass canapés and drinks. I hear this girl used to be a farmer! a host once said to a guest. And I smiled and held out the cocktails and said, yes, I'd farmed apples. When the guest asked me what kind of apples, I told him golden delicious. How marvelous! the guest had said, between sips.

I was grateful for the spoons that needed polishing, the drinks, the plates of food, the trays of sliced cake. For the work that kept my hands busy all the time. I think the people hosting these parties are all the same people, I said once to Mitch when we were cleaning up after a wedding that had gone particularly late. He'd laughed and thrown a bucket of ice onto the landscaped drive. He'd said of course they were always all the same people. How many people do you think can afford shit like this? Not just a massive house, not just gardens, not just a guest house and a pool, but a party, us picking through their hedges at two a.m. for champagne flutes and plates.

Same people or no, it was good money. More money than I'd ever earned before in my life. More than I'd ever even thought about earning. Enough money that paying for the blue room each month was easy. Enough money that it felt like other things could be easy too. Like the money I was earning could maybe be solid enough around me that I wouldn't have to be anything inside of it. Like the money maybe could be just exactly like the arms pressed up against me on the dance floor when I was serving drinks. A kind of scaffolding or carapace, depending on the day.

I made most of my money in tips, from people pressing bills into the front pocket of my vest. When they tipped me, I would smile and hold still. I could have told Mitch, when he interviewed me, about the way that, if someone pushed a bill deep down into the front pocket of my vest, I would smile and say thanks.

You don't have to tell me anything, a man once said to me, draping his flannel shirt around my shoulders when we were out at night. I know what you're thinking, he said. And I didn't have to ask him what? That is to say, I didn't have to test him, to see if he was right. It was a relief too, when he said it. A relief to think that with him, there wasn't anything I had to say or explain.

I barely made it over to the other side of the dance floor before all the drinks were gone. It was a big party, the biggest I'd seen. The champagne was flowing and the people seemed either particularly drunk or particularly on edge, or particularly loose or maybe particularly something else. I'd spent hours anyway making rounds and pouring drinks. It was a big house and guests were constantly popping out of corners and grabbing them off my tray.

When I'd first gotten to the house to set up, I'd been sent out to the garden and asked to weave long-stemmed lilies into small arrangements that could be set out to float in the fountains. Bride's orders, the event coordinator had said, rolling his eyes. There were hyacinths too, huge bouquets of them, that were to be brought out at specific times so that their scent would spill at precise intervals into the air. A dented delivery truck had arrived filled with peacocks and when the driver heaved open the back the birds had come bursting out onto the manicured lawn in a flurry of scaly legs, an explosion of jewel colors and furious beaks.

The man with the flannel shirt used to tell me that I got in my own way, and he would fluff my hair, looking at me in this irresistible way that had just completely taken me in. Get out of your head, he told me when I was worried, and he would tap my temples with his tanned fingers and make me laugh. Now, when I thought about him, I couldn't make sense of the way his words had felt. I supposed it was that his voice had had a kind of rhythm or a special kind of pitch. He knew how to separate out the pieces of me. How to pick out the good and the bad. How to tell me which was which. And who wouldn't fall a little bit in love with a person who could do that? It was why I liked the weddings maybe because all I had to do was follow someone else's plan.

The cake had been brought out in a refrigerated truck and was covered in real gold leaf. We'd set it up on a table at the back of the main tent. There was a way it sparkled, a way it caught the light, that made it seem almost alive. I had learned not to trust a gold like that. I could feel my pulse rise when I passed by it glittering on the table. It was ridiculous, but I couldn't stop the catch in my breath.

When the bride had come to cut it, I almost couldn't watch her because of the color, because of the way it wore all that shimmering foil like skin. When she sunk the knife down through all its golden layers, I shut my eyes. Don't do it, I thought.

The bride had cut the cake alone, without warning or hesitation, standing behind the dancing guests. She hadn't signaled to the event coordinator, or the photographer, she hadn't even looked for her new husband. She'd just walked up to the cake and stuck the knife deep into the bottom tier.

The event coordinator had run into his office then and shut the door, but none of the guests had seemed to mind. They cheered and raised their glasses. Then everyone toasted the bride and called for more champagne.

If any of the guests had thought to whisper among themselves about the missing groom, I didn't hear. They didn't whisper either about the bridesmaid, the pretty blonde one who'd been at the bride's elbow while she said her vows. They only giggled and mouthed things like, absolutely stunning, at each other, while the bride ran her bright red tongue straight up the sugar-crusted knife. Sometimes weddings were wonderful for looking at.

Now it was late though, and I was tired. With the cake cut, there was only dancing left. Bodies coming closer together, arms tangling up, everyone drifting to the beat of a few familiar songs. My vest pocket swelled with bills as I brought around endless rounds of drinks. The hyacinths drooped, and the lilies slipped beneath the surface of the fountains, all the long stems drowned in a hundred slender wrecks. My wrists ached and ached.

I passed by the kitchen on the way back to the bar for more ice. Mitch was wiping out a set of roasting pans. You see how much food came back? he asked. They order so much food at these parties, but no one eats.

Eventually, the pretty bridesmaid was found locked in the upstairs bathroom and one of the servers was called to help her with her dress. A cab was arranged, and she was bundled off through a side door. The bride and groom left the house shortly after through the front. Arm in arm, they walked through the assembled guests, smiling, leaning close, stopping every few steps for a kiss. No one mentioned the lipstick stain on the groom's collar but all the guests craned to look.

With the bride and the groom gone, the party toppled over and collapsed. The guests drained the glasses they were holding and set them down on waiting trays. They kissed the air around each other's faces, everyone agreed that the newlyweds had excellent taste.

Once the guests were gone it all came down to garbage. Collecting it and sorting it and bagging it all up. Glasses had to be counted and ice buckets emptied of ice. Centerpieces and window decorations had to be taken down and put away. Nic found me in the garden pulling a pair of plates out from under one of the kissing benches. She tapped me on the back and asked where I'd been all night.

I was looking for you and looking, she said, but I got stuck taking all these drinks to some lady in the bathroom with a ripped dress. Anyway, she said, it's a long story. These people drink a lot. Are you almost done? Mitch said he'll drive us back when you're ready. Please be ready, she said, pulling me up.

Nic rented one of the basement rooms in Mitch's house. She'd never come along before to help at the parties, but the catering company had called and said they needed extra staff. I had laughed when Nic had come out of her room dressed in my spare work clothes, the flimsy collared shirt, the black polyester pants. I'd promised her I'd help her at the wedding. That I'd show her where to stand, what plates to grab, where to walk, but I'd lost track of her almost right away. Now she was off again, leaving me with the plates. I'll wait for you in the car she said, not bothering to help.

After the plates, there was more garbage and fewer people around to clean it up. I worked for a while in the moonlight, pulling napkins out of bushes and stacking garden chairs. I was fishing a champagne flute out of one of the fountains when Mitch found me. He walked up and wrapped his arms around me and rubbed his stubbled chin against the back of my head.

Leave it, he said. I've got to get out of here. You should have seen the intern they had working with us. Couldn't cook for shit. He spent two hours pitting olives for the tapenade, one by fucking one with this tiny little knife. I thought I was going to have a heart attack just watching him, he said. Mitch smelled like red wine sauce and smoke and roasted bones. Come on, he said, let's get out of here. Everyone else already left.

When we got to his van, we found Nic asleep in the back. I climbed in and Mitch pulled out onto the road, we didn't bother waking her up. I thought about the wedding garbage spilling out onto the perfect grass. The people who hired us cared about the before and the during, how the parties looked, and how they went. They cared that the decorations were on-trend, that the flowers were from the right shops, that the ice was crushed and plentiful, and that we never ran out of canapés or drinks. But they never seemed to care what happened after. If anyone took out the garbage or stayed behind to dry and stack the plates. Who could blame them though if they didn't care about little things like lost deposits? What happened after, after all, was such a grey and boring place.

Thank fuck that's over, said Mitch, as he patted around in his pockets for his cigarettes. There were words tattooed on the backs of his hands and fingers. He'd changed his mind so many times though about what he wanted, that the letters were all just layered blots of ink. It reminded me of those cards doctors sometimes showed to people as a way of finding out what they were thinking. I'd never seen anything though, in the cards or on the back of Mitch's hands. The man with the flannel told me once that I was very tightly shut. I can crack you open like a little walnut though, he'd said, teasing me. He'd said he was so good at his job that I wouldn't feel a thing.

We drove in silence for a long while. The road cutting through olive groves and passing by the sorts of family farms that dotted the hills out in Marin. The honey stalls and jam stands, the places that sold artichokes. It was dark, but I knew the road. I felt the dip of it when we came to the crossing, the farm where I'd picked apples lay just at the end of the road Mitch didn't take.

By the time we got back to Berkeley, the last people still out from the night before were spilling out into the streets. When we got inside the house, we found the grad student who rented one of the bedrooms working on her laptop. Hey Eleni, she said, squinting in the glare from her screen, there was a letter for you taped to the front door. I brought it in when I got back. It looked official, like maybe from the city, only I can't remember where I stuck it now, she said, standing up and sending a pile of books and papers cascading out onto the floor.

It's fine, Mitch said, heading to the kitchen as he worked his way through a last cigarette. Don't worry about it, we're going to bed. We've got to be up early tomorrow morning for another event.

It really was fine. I really was tired, and I really did have to get up early for the next event. But also, I should have asked Katy to find that letter. I should have yelled at her maybe to get up and look for it until it was found, because there were a couple of things that I could think of that a letter from the city might have been about. It was so much easier though to smile and tell her it was fine. To say don't worry about it and to cross my fingers and think maybe it was nothing. Everything was so much easier that way.

I started walking up the stairs to bed, but Katy stopped us. She told us about a party her thesis advisor was throwing for his students. She said he was looking for people to cater it and she'd thought of us. Mitch was saving to open his own restaurant. We'll do it, he said.

Mitch walked up the stairs to his bedroom and I walked up to mine and when I heard him shut his door, I shut mine too. Later, he must have woken up though because he came down the stairs, crawled into my bed and put his arms around me. And maybe it was me using him. Maybe this worked and was a decent way to be. He slipped his hands up underneath my shirt and his fingers were so cool when he touched the marks my bra had made. The divots, the red line drawn around my ribs. Maybe I was using him to unhook me from myself. Letting him untether me a little. Letting him wind me out.

I heard once about some cages and some dogs. How you can make a dog not want to get out, by hurting it when you've locked it in. The person telling me had said that I was like that, like those dogs, but that I didn't have to be.

Those dogs couldn't learn to run away once they'd been broken, he'd told me. And I knew he thought that they were weak and stupid for lying there. And I didn't want him to think that I was weak and stupid too. But I wasn't sure. I thought maybe those dogs knew that the people who were hurting them were the same as the people who were opening the cages. The people that were looking in and smiling, and saying, come on out, you stupid broken dogs, come out. What I think is that those dogs had disappeared. I think that when the people opened the doors, there weren't any dogs left inside those cages anymore to run.

Sometimes I thought this man who had told me about the dogs was like a mirror ground to a fine dust, because sometimes it was like he was all in tiny pieces underneath my skin. Sometimes I thought that when a person looked at me, they saw him there, looking back. I saw him anyway, everywhere. I saw him all the time.

Mitch slid his hands, all the callouses and nicks of them, down my back, and those tattooed ink blots spread out all over the top of me. It's hard to be myself, was something I'd said once to that other man, the dog one, the man with the soft flannel shirt. And he'd said, it doesn't have to be. And how could it be wrong to love someone who says a thing like that?

four months before the trial

Ari

I didn't know Lucy very well even though she'd lived next door since she was born, in the house with the green shutters and the trees that were always all year dumping needles on our roof. I almost never saw her come outside. My mom thought maybe Lucy had issues, and she made me laugh when she said it. Issues. Because she said it all whispered and with her face wide and snapping open just like blinds. And she made me want to say, what? And be laughing, all lightly in giggling disbelief but also it made me rear up inside myself like a horse, like those tall, muscled thoroughbreds. The way they are when they come out of the gate, their eyes all wide and rolling, chest heaving and foaming at the mouth.

Lucy was funny though. When I got to know her, I liked the way she sometimes put her arms around me and said I had cheesy, garlic breath. The way she sometimes told me and kept telling me to brush my teeth. Brush your teeth, she said to me sometimes when I came over. Ari, she sometimes said, coming right up close and leaning in, your breath, it's disgusting. Go and brush your teeth. But the way that she would say it was teasingly, like I was an outgoing person, like we were both on the same side of the joke.

On Tuesdays, I ate peanut butter sandwiches. On Wednesdays, I ate almond butter ones. On Thursdays it was back to peanut butter, and so on. The days were numbered off like that. Peanut butter and then almond butter, back and forth. This was supposed to mimic flexibility when it came to sandwiches. Like I could have either on any day, or even both. Mom made them in front of me as per an agreement we'd worked out, where I watched her measure and spread the prescribed two tablespoons of filling onto slices of whole-wheat bread. The therapist I was driven to on Fridays talked about adding tuna. Tuna sandwiches are lovely, she said.

She said that tuna sandwiches would be progress. A step in the right direction. I said I'd think about it. Which shouldn't have been a surprise to her really, girls like me lie all the time.

Lee once said it to me outright, while I was up on a ladder checking on a tinkling cluster of tiny apples, turning them and polishing their skin. Girls like you are liars, was what he said. And maybe he was teasing us like he sometimes liked to do but also, he was right. Girls like me are liars, we lie about things all the time. Was tuna fish lovely? Would it make me a better, more well-adjusted person if I ate it? I was a liar, so how could I know.

I liked to lean against the counter while Mom drank coffee and made my sandwiches. While she measured and spread and smooshed. If everything was going well and smooth between us, if everything was right and clear and if we were also careful, we could joke a little about the process. It was a bit like that in the mornings, each of us trying to gauge when it might be alright to laugh.

She dropped me off at the library on her way to work, then she came back to watch me eat my sandwich at one o'clock and again at four o'clock to watch me while I ate my snack. Dinner was at seven or seven thirty, but we would be home by then. Sometimes, her friend came to watch me if she was busy at work.

I ate on the benches outside the library, in front of my mom or my mom's friend. The friend was always knitting hats to donate to the hospital for premature babies, her needles would go click click click and I would time the sound to my chewing for a game. If she dropped a stitch she'd say damn, and then she'd tell me not to tell my mother that she'd said that. Your mom will think I'm a bad influence, she would say, smoothing her ice-cream-coloured pants. Forgetting maybe that I wasn't a kid anymore. Forgetting maybe that I was twenty. That I could have been doing so many other things. That I could have been working or finishing college or thinking about graduate school. There were so many other things that I could have been doing besides chewing there with my face turned toward her so she could see I wasn't spitting anything out.

After I finished my sandwich, and after I'd shown my mom or my mom's friend the empty wrapper (with no cheating crumbs of bread or globs of peanut butter or almond butter in it), I'd throw away the paper lunch bag and write in my notebook that I kept to show the doctor. One peanut butter sandwich, I'd write. Or, I'd write the same thing only I'd say almond butter. Then I'd write two slices, whole-wheat bread. If there was fruit, I'd write that there was fruit. One apple, I'd write and then I'd write if it was red or green. The therapist said that I could also write down my feelings. That would be wonderful, she said, don't you think? Which made me realize she wasn't really listening to anything I said.

There were things that I did want to write though, on the papers I was keeping for the doctor. I wanted to write that I'd been enrolled in a women's studies degree and I wondered if it was funny that I'd dropped out essentially because I was having trouble being a woman myself.

I wanted to write, Foucault argued that the body is a social construct, right next to apple, in the boxes where I recorded my meals. Or sometimes, I wanted to write, this disorder is the inescapable result of a misogynistic society! Which was something I'd read once in a book and underlined without really all-the-way believing it. Anyway, it's hard to think of yourself as nothing but a consequence or a negative result.

Next to my weekly meal plans I wanted to write, why are the bodies of women and girls marked as deviant if they fail to conform? And also, I wanted to confess how amazing, how rewarding conforming sometimes felt. I wanted to ask my doctor if she'd ever worn a tight dress or a really short skirt. I wanted to tell her how people smiled at me more when I didn't eat. How they held doors open for me and looked after me and let me go first and win at games. And I wanted to write, how can we trust a patriarchal society to diagnose or treat us? next to where I had written, almond butter, two tablespoons. I wanted to write it all out.

Really, I wanted to be able to write in my food journal that I wasn't at home, in my old bedroom, sleeping in my childhood bed. That I wasn't eating on benches outside the library and writing it down.

After lunch, I would go back into the library and sit on the beanbag chairs in the teen section. There I would read magazines and watch the clock and wait until it was four, which made it time for me to go out to the benches and eat my snack. When Mom got off work she'd pick me up. At home I would eat dinner and write that down and then we would watch TV, or I would sit in my room on my bed. At ten, Mom would duck her head around my door, and wish me goodnight.

Sometimes Mom would ask if I wanted to borrow the car. Do you want to borrow the car? she would ask me. Or she would say, you should go out. My friends were all at college getting on with things. That was part of what we weren't talking about when Mom made my sandwiches or when she packed my snacks. Or when I watched her put butter (one tablespoon) or sour cream (two tablespoons) on my potatoes at dinner and I was suddenly like one of those hunting dogs that smells a deer in the woods. That is to say taut and switched-on and filled up to the neck in an instant with streaming wildness. When she watched me write in my journal for the doctor or when she offered me the car, what we weren't doing was talking about any of that.

It was January when I started babysitting Lucy. Where I'd been before, where I'd spent the past spring and summer, where I'd gone while my friends had stayed in college, was one of the other things we didn't talk about. It was often very quiet between us in the house.

Lucy wasn't quiet though. She liked to talk. Most of all, she liked to talk about diving and second of all, she liked to talk about environments. Atmosphere, she would have said. I found this out, her first most liked topic, and her second, as soon as I started going over to her house to babysit her while her mom worked nights.

That poor woman, my mom would say about Lucy's mom, spreading almond butter or peanut butter right to the edges of a piece of bread, or counting out the seven pretzels that went into my snack. Her husband left last year while you were gone, my mom would say, licking the salt from her fingers if there was salt. Just left! Can you believe it? One day he just walked out. I saw him dragging a suitcase out the door and carrying this little plastic trash can under one arm. A trash can! And now Alison's working nights, my mom would say, finishing, by then always almost breathless. Can you imagine? That poor woman, she would say again, shaking her head and slipping the butter knife, if there was a butter knife, between her teeth.

This was gone over many times. The leaving. The suitcase. The trash can. The, and now she's working nights! It was gone over while we were making sandwiches and watching sandwiches be made. Or counting pretzels and watching them be counted. Or driving and watching drive. Or grocery shopping and watching shop (I didn't like to hold the basket or push the cart, but I liked to be there at the store to see that the right things were being bought). We often talked about Alison, the poor woman, and Lucy, the daughter that maybe had issues. We talked about how strange it must be in their house with Lucy's dad now gone from it. In that horrible way! my mom would say, shaking her head.

We were always thinking about that house, maybe, is one way to put it. That other house that must be so different, that must be so quiet now with one less person there. That house with its pine-needle-clogged roof and the cracked shingles growing moss. That house hiding underneath those rampant, ill-tended trees.

Lucy's babysitter quit one afternoon in those long hours that dragged between snack time and dinner time when I did nothing usually but lie on my bed. Mom came bursting into my room to tell me. I talked to Alison just now! Out in the driveway! She looked so tired! She really did, the poor thing. She had these terrible dark circles under her eyes! It's not surprising, working like she does. Anyway, the babysitter quit with no warning! And it's not like Alison can just take the night off! I told her you wouldn't mind watching Lucy, my mom said. You should have seen how relieved she was! She says there's a room you can sleep in over at her house. She says you don't need to bring anything. All you have to do is keep Lucy company and she'll be home in the morning. How about it? she said, opening one of my dresser drawers and pulling out my pyjamas and putting them in a bag for me along with a hairbrush.

Besides, my mom said, it'll be good for you to get out of the house. You can eat your dinner here and then you can go over, she said. That night I was having a potato with two tablespoons of sour cream, two cups of vegetables and a protein shake. I'd been thinking about it all afternoon, wondering if the potato would be fluffy on the inside. If I would season it with both pepper and salt.

Remember to be careful around Lucy, my mom said when I was leaving, you don't know what might set her off. Another person in another family, another me with another mother, might have said, look at me writing two tablespoons of sour cream in my neat handwriting. Look at me doing this and then ask who should be careful around whom. But also, I appreciated that she thought that I could do it. That she thought that I could be a person writing down two tablespoons of sour cream and also someone who might be able to take care of someone else.

I had taken very good care of some apple trees, the year before, when I had been away. And though I had tried to tell her about the trees and about my taking care of them, she had stopped me. Let's just put all that behind us, she said. Honestly, she said, it doesn't bear thinking about.

I'd tried to tell my therapist too, about the trees. I'd told her they were strange, the trees that I'd been taking care of. That they weren't like any other apple trees I'd ever seen. I'd said they looked old, but that their bark was smooth and warm when you touched it, like skin. I'd said that the girls that were being treated there were asked sometimes to climb up long ladders and polish the little apples with soft cloths so they could catch the light. But my therapist had only huffed and said what a thing to let girls like us do. Honestly, she said, I don't know what that man was thinking, I read about it in the paper. What happened there, she said.

When I went over to Lucy's house that first night, Alison showed me the spare room. It was right next to Lucy's. She can put herself to bed, Alison said. Lucy's pretty self-sufficient. You're here mostly just in case. But can you make her breakfast? In the morning? I'll be back around nine or so, she said, depending on when I can get off. Can you cook? she said, looking at me.

Sure, I said, I could do that.

I asked her if I needed to get Lucy ready for school. Lucy doesn't go to school, Alison said. She said it wasn't the right sort of place for her, that Lucy was better off at home. Anyway, she said, thanks so much, it's a huge help, coming last minute like this.

After Alison left, I went to Lucy's room and knocked on the door. A girl dressed in two or three sweatshirts and wrapped also in two or three scarves opened the door. She was almost as tall as me, it was hard to believe that she was only twelve.

Hi, I said, I'm Ari, from next door. She stared at me but didn't answer. Eventually, she put the end of one of her scarves into her mouth. I said, I'm going to stay here tonight with you. Is that alright?

She took the scarf out of her mouth and asked what I knew about cave diving. I said I didn't know anything about cave diving and she hmphed and shoved the damp end of the scarf back in her mouth. She held a pipette in her hand, which dripped on the floor while she stood looking at me. Then she left the doorway and went over to a wall of tanks teeming with underwater plants. With her back to me, she started squeezing drops into the tanks, counting under her breath.

I'm interested in atmosphere, she said after a minute. Then she said, atmosphere is different than environment! As if I'd made some remark, said somehow that they were the same thing. I nodded though and said, of course.

She was awkward in the way she moved inside her scarves and sweatshirts and in the way she talked, which was too loud, as if she were the only one in the room. She probably usually was, I thought. Environment you can step away from, she said. Environment you can get out of. But atmosphere is different. Atmosphere is what you breathe. Atmosphere is the environment that you take inside yourself.

I like these plants because I can see if I'm getting their atmosphere right, she told me. I can tell by their leaves. By the color of them, their quality of green. Most places, she said, putting the pipette down in a tray on her crowded desk, are poisonous. Most places start out toxic and stay that way. Did you know that? she said, coming over and standing very close to me.

Did you know that the air you're breathing right now would kill you if you tried to breathe it underwater? I told her I didn't know that but she didn't give any sign that she'd heard.

I'm in training to be a cave diver, she continued. I'm growing these plants now but when I'm old enough, it's going to be me underwater. When I'm old enough, it's going to be me dropping down and exploring the deep caves by myself and breathing the right sort of air.

I looked around and saw that her room was piled high with books. What do you like to read? I asked her but she ignored the question. You smell like peanut butter, she said instead. Or, no, maybe almond butter, startling me into a laugh.

Later, after she had brushed her teeth, I stopped in the doorway of her room and turned off the light. Come and find me if you need anything, I said, not expecting her to respond. I thought maybe even that she might already be asleep, so I was surprised when she said that indeed, there might be something I could do. But first, she said she had to know if I could work in the dark. If I didn't mind it. Do you mind the dark? she asked. And because I wanted her to go to sleep, I said I could. I don't mind it, I said.

I turned to go, but she kept talking. She needed to know she told me, because she was training to be a cave diver. A deep cave diver of the most extreme and risk-taking variety. I'm talking two hundred meters down, she said. I'm talking about swimming deep underwater for hours and hours. She wanted to know if I could handle that.

And because I wanted her to go to sleep, I said, sure. Absolutely. Two hundred meters down, I said. Hours and hours. I could do that.

OK then, she said. I think you can help me out.

Sometimes when you have been deep inside a thing, so deep down that you can no longer see the exits, or the way that you came to be there even in the first place, to get out of that place, to move forward, you have to take a chance.

Lee told us we were liars, but he also taught us that. That to go forward, we would have to let ourselves go. Even if that meant we couldn't really see what was coming or what would happen next. He told us that if we wanted to get better, we'd have to let someone lead us out.

We did want to get better, didn't we? he asked us. He said that we'd been holding on to a rope, but that that rope, in the end, was our sickness. He said to get better, we would have to trust him, that we would have to let go. And I had felt at the time some hesitation, and he must have seen it because he said, that's it, that's your sickness welling up inside you. That's your sickness telling you not to trust me, not to listen to the things I say. You have to let that go, he said. That sick, mistrusting thing inside of you. Girls like you are always lying, he said, but there's no one that you lie to more often than yourselves. I didn't feel like I was lying to Lucy when I told her I'd go down diving with her. But that was the thing about lying I supposed, I was so used to it, I did it all the time.

I got to like spending the night at Lucy's and I got to like being her babysitter too. As the months went on, I started sleeping at least five nights a week over at her house. I slept better there anyway than I did in my own room, tucked up in the little twin bed, listening to the quiet bubbling of Lucy's tanks. I learned to make Lucy breakfast just the way she liked it, two scrambled eggs, with packets of sugar broken over the top like salt. I was good at it I guess is what I mean to say. At taking care of her.

When I told her about it, my therapist said of course you're good at cooking for other people. Girls like you usually are, she said. But cooking for other people is not productive, it's not the direction we want to take, she said. But I was making eggs for Lucy like Lee had made eggs for us. I was doing things right over the top of him maybe. Inviting memories of him into the room with me and trying them out.

Lee cooked us eggs in the mornings. He would crack them one-handed into the cast iron pan he rubbed each day with oil and salt. No one knew how to cook eggs the right way, he'd tell us. No one took the time. Some outpatient programs made you eat pizza, to see if you were well enough to leave. Someone or other would come by with a slice from the hospital cafeteria, and if you could eat it, they'd tick a box that said you had made progress or even could be released.

So when Lee stopped us in the mornings at the kitchen table just before we took a bite, when he told us to wait because he hadn't put on the salt, and when he crushed the flakes between his index finger and thumb and rained them down just so delicately right onto the warm yolks, that was something that I hadn't seen before.

There were other things though. He was slippery, I had to break Lee down into pieces to get him right. I just wanted the man with blue eyes who could cook perfect eggs and who gave us good advice. But that wasn't all of it. That wasn't the whole picture. That was me lying about it all over again to myself.

I moved some things from my house into Lucy's and I began to like standing in her doorway and listening to her talk about her underwater plants. I began to like sitting on her bed, not saying anything, just looking at the perfect greens of her sunken ferns and vines. There was a kind of stillness I was finding with her. She loved to tell me about diving. And I began to like to listen too. I have always been a good listener, I hear that girls like me usually are.

By March, I had started spending days with Lucy too. I liked whispering with her through the afternoons while Alison slept. It was so quiet in her house that I could hear across the way sometimes when the phone rang in mine. Which was how I got the call I lied about and said I hadn't gotten. Later, when I was asked. When it was all quite serious and it was all, Miss, we did contact you. And I was all, what? With my heart racing.

That was later though, just before the trial. In March, when I picked up the phone, it was just an assistant. Just gathering information. Just a cheerful voice saying, is this

Ari Nix? I'd like to ask you some questions if that's alright.

And then it was just me lying and lying and saying that I didn't know a thing about it. And then it was just me bringing the phone down from my ear like nothing at all was wrong. And then it was my knees giving out right underneath me and me dropping down to the floor. After that, I didn't answer the phone when I heard it ringing. I stayed at Lucy's house and we talked about diving. I liked it better, I told myself, there at Lucy's house, away from mine.

Sometimes I borrowed Alison's car and drove Lucy to the library. Lucy knew the librarians there because they ordered books for her. They ordered anything she wanted, diving records from university collections, manuals or copies of hand-drawn charts. Once, we got an envelope stuffed with loose notes, just speculations on what the diver had felt with her hands down there in the cold dark.

We liked to read the books at the library right when they came in. Sitting together, elbow to elbow at the big table by the reference desk. My mom started making sandwiches for Lucy too and we ate them when she came at one o'clock. Afterwards, we wrote down what we had eaten in the journals that we both now kept. Our logbooks Lucy called them. All divers have them, she told me, writing seriously, keeping careful track. She told me all divers knew how important it was to take notes.

Two slices of bread, we wrote. Two tablespoons of almond butter or peanut butter, depending. Apple, we wrote, noting down if it was red or green. When we ate, we practiced chewing carefully and taking very small bites. Like divers do underwater, Lucy told my mom, who would have come from the office and who would already be running late. Could you two just hurry up? my mom would say, looking at her watch.

Lucy would explain that we couldn't. Divers have to be able to chew their food underwater without choking, she said. And that means we have to take extremely small bites. We could be down there twelve or more hours, Lucy told her, explaining. If we don't chew very slowly, we could get a leak in our masks.

We took calculated sips of water and we marked that down too in our logbooks. The water, the small sips of it. It's a serious business, trying to keep yourself alive underwater, Lucy said. And I said I believed it, that I knew.

I loved it, chewing slowly for the dives. Come on Mom, I'd say, teasing her. We're practicing, we have to eat like this to stay alive. That was how Mom stopped coming to eat with us. She stopped coming, but we still ate the sandwiches and wrote it down. Like we were really divers. Like we were already underwater. And this to me, this keeping eating, was new. I tried not to look at it too closely or think too much about what sort of thing it was. Lee said we wouldn't know what getting better was at first, when getting better was first happening to us. I wondered if this was it.

After we finished our sandwiches, we liked to close our eyes and stick our hands under the bench. We liked to run our fingers along the underside of it, bumping them over all the bits of sticky garbage, the wet spots, the sharp spots, the crusted wads of gum. We weren't waiting for instructions. We were making our own plans.

When we weren't practicing our underwater eating, we read books about swimming through caves. We read about how our bodies would slow down when we were deep underwater. How everything would stretch to only the infinity of here and now. We read about what it would feel like to drop deeper and deeper through water, down long shafts that might open suddenly beneath the rocks.

The Greeks thought that you would have to fall for nine days to get to Tartarus. To me, it had always seemed like a kind of promise, that after nine days of falling you would arrive at a different place. A below place of caves and quietness. When Lucy said, we'll go so deep down, I sometimes thought, nine days. The opening to Tartarus was underwater. A tiny hole, the size of a bottle's neck.

This is what it will be like, Lucy sometimes whispered to me, pointing to pictures or to passages in her books. The parts where people went further, or stayed under longer, or swam alone through caves that no one had ever swum through before. Two hundred meters down, she said. Imagine going two hundred meters down and never coming to the bottom. Imagine what that would feel like.

I had been somewhere the year before. And I thought, nine days down. And I thought about a bottle's neck. And I thought yes, I could imagine it.

four months before the trial

Hesper

It was almost time to get off, only five minutes more to time-to-go, so everything was starting to go greatly woozy and soft as a mole's snout. All dark blues and sinking purples and silky-smooth leggy round numbers. All twos and fours and sixes coiling. All small thoughts and small muscles almost all relaxing. The minutes were ticking me softly over, five, then four and so on. Just pushing me so gently and rocking me like a little breeze.

Things were about to be good. Things were about to relax. Now there was breath-holding and now there was tightness but not for so much longer. Soon I could leave the library reference desk and I would be back in my apartment underneath my brown and yellow blankets. Everything was sliding, dumping now all rightly and directly down towards evening. I could feel it, the softness, and the quietness of it coming down so closely now and brushing me, all feathers and wings.

The girl sitting next to me behind the desk, Sarah or Sasha or Sam or Samantha, something that started with an S, was watching skincare videos on her phone. Glue-eyed and rapt and me too, the both of us watching, as she tapped on one little face after another. Like a daisy chain all threaded stem to stem, but only instead of little flowers it was an endless chain of perfect pores. All smooth noses, and tiny chins and lips.

We couldn't see the girls mostly, not the girls as they were themselves, the all of them together but only just the bits of them that were getting smooth and soft. Only just the creamy morsels of them and I couldn't stop myself from bumping my chapped fingers over my own unperfected cheeks. From running them just quickly over all the little places that I'd picked at and all the places I might pick at just a little more if I only paused or gave myself even half a chance. But I wasn't picking, and it was almost time to go, and soon I would be in my apartment and for now we were just squeaking in our chairs and for now we were just tapping our feet against the ground and for now we were just straightening our skirts and letting the minutes pass.

The other girl snapped her gum and tapped another video. She picked at the end of her long ponytail and one of my hands bolted up my sleeve and brushed a scab on the inside of my arm and then I had to freeze and close my eyes and bite my lip but not too hard and count to ten. It was what Lee had taught us. Not the biting bit, but the freezing and counting, and the holding very still to keep calm. We had practiced in his living room after breakfast, making ourselves still and cold all over, frozen just like blocks of ice. Counting slowly after eating and listening to the sound of his voice.

My fingers though were getting hot, and Lee wasn't with me, and I wasn't living anymore in his house. Behind the reference desk, my skin was getting tighter and tighter and starting to itch. The minutes were ticking down but not fast enough and then, disaster. A student came up to the desk with a long list of items to request. Then he was handing it to me and there was only just one minute now to go until I was supposed to leave.

And that was it. It was like that sometimes, the tipping over. The hard white hitch of it just hitting me and shoving me off. I smiled wide at the student though and asked him just like I was supposed to, how it was that I could help. But I was toppling over off my calm and centered and I was teetering over the edge of an abyss. The clock was ticking and it was suddenly quite absolutely grave and desperate. So I found the scab that I had touched before and picked it off. And it was all stars then and oozing and all then such clean, bright relief.

Then it wasn't though. Because Lee was there, the part of him that clung to me and spread around me like an oil slick. Oh, he said, chuckling, I knew you would do that. I knew you wouldn't make it to time-to-get-off. I knew something would happen, he said.

The only thing to do was to ignore him. To talk to the student and to pretend like I couldn't hear Lee. No one else can see you, I told him, sliding my hand out of my sleeve. But Lee said it didn't matter, he only cared about me.

I made my face calm and cool like mint green jelly and held my hand out to the student, ready to take his list, but there on the end of my finger all obvious and dangling was the crusted yellow top of the scab. Lee saw it as soon as I did and the student saw it too and we all three stared at it together for a moment, until Lee toppled over laughing and rolled down the whole length of my back. And he was howling and doubled over and saying, just look at how you're managing without me. Oh, just look at how well you're getting on. And he was giggling and burrowing down deep into my back pocket. Oh lord, he said, it's just too much.

There was nothing I could do but wipe my hand and take the paper from the student and smile and tell him absolutely, that we would do our best to help.

So, is that OK? the real and actually quite nice-looking student said, in his real, and nice-sounding and not in-my-own-head nice-sounding voice. Seeing, maybe, how I had then quickly gone away for just that second, like a girl in a magic trick, like blink and I'm sawed in half, chopped-up or gone. He had blonde hair, the real true person. A small cloud of it, dusted with something orange. You can get them for tomorrow? he asked. The papers and things?

We'll try our best, I told him, trying to shoo Lee away.

Oh god thanks, the student said, he told me he'd come back the next day to check. And I nodded all serenely like cool swans gliding and waited in the chair behind the desk for him to go. Just as soon as he disappeared down in the stacks though, I stuffed his list into my pocket and took off almost leaping up the stairs. Lee came with me, flapping up beside me, laughing about the way I was sweating through my shirt. Didn't I teach you anything? he asked me. All this over just three minutes late? And he tutted at me and said I must be disappointed, to be still like this. Maybe it's time you came back and saw me, he said.

My apartment was what had once been the back hallway of an old house, chopped up now into studios. There wasn't a lot of space. If I pulled the oven door all the way down for instance, it touched the cabinet screwed into the wall on the other side. But still, it was my apartment and I was an official tenant with an official landlord named Dave. Dave had wedged an old clawfoot tub into the bathroom and a deep tub was all I really needed anyway to be at home. A good bathtub, to someone with skin like mine, is a gift and I floated away just all my evenings in it after work. Soaking right up to my neck in water as hot as I could get it, all fuzzed out and towel-soft and warm.

I drew a bath and sprinkled in some oatmeal and took the pills I was supposed to take. Lee wasn't there because he didn't care so much when I was doing the right things. Sometimes though I wished he'd come around. Sometimes when it was so quiet and it was only me in the apartment I missed him and wished that he was there.

Later, I crawled all pink and scrubbed into the brown and yellow blankets I kept piled up on the brown and yellow bed. The bed was a gift to me from the last tenant, which is to say the last tenant had left it along with sheets and pillows and a few garbage bags full of clothes. The last tenant had also left three Hershey bars and six Snickers rolled up in the blankets but I'd eaten those right away, so they were gone. When I woke it was morning and someone was knocking on the door.

It must have been quite late because the sun was streaming right in through the blinds. The someone had moved on to rattling the doorknob and calling out to see if anyone was there. I had to freeze and count to ten and pretend that I was out because there were surely things that might bring people to the door of my apartment, but those were things I didn't want to talk to anyone about.

When the knocking stopped, I swept the floor and that was tidying and that was doing the right things and getting the right things done. Then I made myself some instant coffee and let the world drag itself together while I sipped. I put my phone on silent though and slid it down into the drawer beside the sink just to be safe.

No one is coming, Lee said to us sometimes, the year before. No one else is coming to save you from this, he would tell us if one or another one of us was scared or crying about something we had to eat. Sometimes he would be silly about it and make us laugh. He would peek out the window above the sink and slide open the curtains and say, see? No one's there.

No one is coming, he'd say to one of us if we were crying over a plate of pancakes or bacon or scrambled eggs. And if we could laugh about it, it would be over. And it would just be pancakes. Only things lying all so still and harmless on our plates, and Lee would say, trust me, and he would rest his hand on our shoulders and tell us that he could pull us out of this. All we had to do was listen he told us, all we had to do was exactly what he said. Easy, he said, easy. All we had to do was take a bite.

Something rapped hard on the door of my apartment and I dropped my coffee and the bile rose right up my throat and for a minute and then another minute, I couldn't move. The year before, when I'd lived in his house, if I'd been scratching, Lee would have stopped me. Or if I couldn't move, he'd have come and picked me up. I waited there all quiet and shallow-breathing for quite a while, listening and listening but the knocking at the door didn't come again.

8 hours before the trial

Ari

A bright flash of ankle and Eleni was in. And for a moment it was all swish and hum, like a wave when you go under, like how the water can go as hard as concrete right when your head hits. For a moment it was all the heady smell of young apples dropping. That musk that just seeps out of them when they're green and unripe and rotten all at once. When they're too hard and too soft and sick. There was too the wave of my own blood rising, and the tinkling of the little golden blossoms chiming softly in the dead night air. But there was surely no Eleni.

The door swung shut behind her and she was somewhere in that house. And then it wasn't just the smell of apples, because then I was afraid. And I was suddenly as thin as paper, all just crawling skin and stomach dropping down and ice. I hissed out between my teeth at Eleni, at the place she had been standing just before.

You said we wouldn't go inside, I told the back of her. The closed door of her. The patch of her where she'd just been. There were tears now coming too because I could see that she'd been lying to us. And I had sometimes been a liar too, but I hadn't thought that she would lie to me. She'd promised me and Hesper that we wouldn't go inside. She promised us we'd only come to look.

I'd tried to grab her when she'd started inching closer to the house. When we'd only just been out in the garden. When we'd only just been laughing with the wild thrill of being back, but not really back. Of being there but not staying, of taking a peek.

I'd felt her tipping towards the house though, and I'd

reached out to catch her, thinking it was just an accident. Just a trick of the trees or the shadows or the light. But I'd felt suddenly a little sick and my skin had pricked in an instant, all sweat and little hairs like hackles telling me that I should not be there. And I saw it, how the whole night she'd been leading us right up to the door. How the whole night she'd been planning to go back inside the house. How maybe she'd just needed us to watch her go.

I saw then what I hadn't seen when we'd met up at the hotel. When I had been distracted, ecstatic just to see her so suddenly there in front of me after I had missed her for so long. I saw the way she'd let the garden creep back up inside her while we had been away. How she hadn't kept it off her, how she hadn't been fastidious. How she'd let it grow back right underneath her skin. And now there was Hesper sinking down beside me. Like, with Eleni gone, there was nothing left to hold her up.

I tried to hold Hesper tight against me, but she only slipped and whispered it was wrong. Eleni lied to us, she said. And she pulled at her hair and sunk her fingernails into the soft sides of her cheeks. Her teeth were chattering together. Ari, she said, crouching down beside me now like maybe she was going to be sick, this isn't what it was supposed to be like.

Eleni was in the house though, and we couldn't reach inside to bring her back. Even so, we called to her. Even so, we said, Eleni. Through the front window we could see her. She was looking, like we were, into the waiting darkness of the house.

Maybe we thought that we could stop him from coming. Stop him somehow from getting close. He was there though. He was there and coming towards her from the kitchen. Moving softly, like he always did, padding in his slippers, wearing that soft flannel shirt. Hesper shivered and we couldn't look away. She said he was just the way that she remembered him, and she was right. He was just the way that he had been.

Eleni used to say that Lee was like a toenail. You can rip him out, she said, but he'll just grow back. And Hesper and I had giggled when she said it, but also it made us uneasy to think about. Uneasy because we knew that it was worse even than what she said. We knew that it wasn't just that he'd grow back that made him like a toenail, but that your skin would keep a bed ready for him while he was gone.

We said we wouldn't go inside, Hesper said. We said we only came to look. But of course, driving there, we must have suspected something. Hesper and me, we had that deep-cut nail bed carved out for Lee inside us too. You could see it, even then, even in the dark, even after all that time, how it was grooved and pocked and obvious just behind our eyes and on our skin. The way we wanted too to just be near him. The way we wanted still to hear the things he had to say. You could see it written right across our faces in the moonlight, the way we kept a place for him just puckered up inside ourselves, all stripped bare-naked and laid out.

Early on in my time in his house, when I was sitting in the kitchen after breakfast, Lee told me something he told all the girls when they first arrived. Do you know, he said, about a thing called inescapable shock? He was brushing his warm knuckles over the back of my hand. Not touching me, not really, but only pricking up the little hairs when he came close, while Hesper washed the dishes just behind me, up to her elbows in soapy water in the sink. When I shook my head, he'd smiled and settled back in his chair. Well, let me tell you about it then, he'd said. And he'd started to talk about a couple of scientists that had done a research project that involved giving dogs electric shocks.

Eleni though, listening from another room, had interrupted. Oh not that again, she'd said and laughed. Not that again Lee, she'd said. Not all that about the dogs. Lee had looked at me from under his wiry eyebrows and twinkled his blue eyes in my direction. Just like we maybe had a secret, like can you believe I have to deal with this? And sometimes it was really like that in his house. Sometimes it was really easy. Sometimes you could feel caught up and warm and like you were special and being shown a thing.

Well, Lee said, his eyes still sparkling and crinkling, right at the edges, like he was letting me in on a joke, the scientists put the dogs in locked cages. And they found that if they shocked the dogs enough, they could unlock the cages and shock the dogs again and they wouldn't try to run away. Even with the doors wide open and nothing holding them back. The dogs would just lie there inside the cages, Lee said smiling. They wouldn't move. Other dogs, dogs that hadn't been restrained before and shocked before, would bolt if the scientists tried to hurt them. But these dogs, he said, pinching up his lips the way he did when he was thinking, these dogs that had been locked up first and shocked, they didn't try to get away.

There are some moments that stay right inside of you without becoming different or better or changing a bit. Little blistered pockets of present-and-eternal tucked away inside of you like gravel, all tender and distended just underneath the skin. Maybe it wasn't that those shocked dogs didn't know how to run away. Maybe they knew more than the scientists did about how things worked. Maybe the dogs knew that there are kinds of cages you have to stay in once you'd been inside. Maybe the dogs knew about that.

I might have asked Lee about that, about whether there were cages that you couldn't walk out of even if the door was hanging open. Whether there were cages where walking out of them would have been beside the point. But Hesper dropped the plate that she was drying and it broke and Lee looked up at her so fast his glasses slipped. He was still smiling when he looked up, but his eyes traveled slowly between Hesper and the plate. And it seemed like something bad was maybe about to happen. Except there was Eleni, running right into the kitchen, stepping between Hesper and Lee. And she was so light and warm and laughing. And she was brushing the backs of my shoulders with her little fingers and saying, oh god you three what is it now? and everything settled and was fine.

Later, Lee sometimes talked about obedience. How it was important for us to follow rules in a place like this. And of course, we knew that because we'd all been to other places. When it came to recovery, this wasn't our first attempt. He taught me how to French a rack of lamb right at the kitchen table. How to slide the knife in between the connective tissue. How to pull the bones out cleanly with my fingers, all glistening and white. And he'd said, see? If you hadn't stuck the knife in where I showed you, you might have cut your finger. You can't imagine how sharp this knife is, he said. But I didn't need to worry, because I was a good listener, and good listeners, he told me, don't get hurt.

At first though we weren't doing any cutting, it was just the story about the dogs and the little hairs tingling on my wrist. At first it was just breakfast at his table, just Eleni laughing and the broken dish.

Then Eleni wasn't in the window and Hesper grabbed my arm again and twisted the skin of it and said, I can't see her. I can't see Eleni. Where's she gone? Hesper was asking like maybe we didn't know. But we did know where Eleni had gone, and knowing made it worse.

We'd only just been peeking in the windows, only just stumbled half-drunk out of the taxi and come down the long drive. We'd only just been back at the hotel. Eleni had only just been grabbing both our hands and saying we should go. We should go out and see the house right now, she said. While we still can, she whispered. Before the trial starts. Hesper said we shouldn't, that we couldn't, that we surely weren't allowed, that anyway it was the middle of the night. But we were all already pulling on our coats and calling reception and asking if they might please call us a cab.

It had felt so much like the right thing to do, sitting together in the back seat. Just leaning into each other and letting the car take us out into the warm night. We told the driver where to go and Eleni rolled down the window and smiled the way we remembered her smiling the year before. The way she hadn't been, back at the hotel. Which is to say she had her real smile out, where her eyes got sharp and we could see her teeth. And she had leaned forward and told the driver to go faster, and she had grabbed our hands and we had felt the heat radiating out from her palms.

When we'd gotten to the crossing, Eleni had pressed a wad of bills into the driver's hand. He'd hesitated, but she'd stopped him, saying, yes, this is definitely it. Thank you, she told him, just drop us here. He'd asked us if we wanted him to wait, but she'd said no. And Hesper had said, wouldn't it be better if he stayed? Wouldn't we all like for him to leave the engine running and the doors unlocked and maybe even just cracked a little open for us if we needed to get in quickly? But Eleni had only laughed and said no, of course not, a car waiting for us would ruin the mood.

And her eyes had been so big and shiny and she had seemed so suddenly light. And she'd been so pretty in the moonlight, and she'd told the driver that really, he could leave. And then it had been just so deadly quiet and so dark we couldn't see a thing. But Eleni had been smiling and smiling, and all around us had been the smell of it, those old trees, that thick ripeness – Lee's garden, all that intoxicating fruit.

We were back, and in the end it had been easy. Like we'd been running uphill for months, not knowing we could just have turned around. And suddenly we weren't weighed down by what had happened but only pulled hard by the wild joy of careening off the tracks. And it had been just like the year before, with Lee's old van parked by the apple tree out front. The branch of it was still lying in front of the house, so ugly and so enormously dead, the side of the tree still gaping like we'd only just then heard it crack. We wanted it, didn't we? Somehow, we wanted it, what happened next.

We should leave, Hesper said. But Eleni was inside so we weren't going back to the hotel. We crept up to the fallen branch and slowly edged our way around it towards the back of the house. He can't see us, Hesper whispered, knowing we both thought that maybe he could. We heard Eleni laughing from inside the kitchen and we knew the way Lee would have been circling. Heating the oven and turning on the gas.

Lee had a thing about seeing us. He could always do it. In the mornings, just like in any treatment program, we'd be weighed and measured. And just like anywhere, if we were asked to in these check-ins, we'd untie our hospital gown, and show a shoulder. Or lift our shirt, if we were allowed to wear our normal clothes, and show our backs. Or it would be our thighs or the insides of our arms. Or any patch of skin that we'd had trouble with, that we'd worried at or damaged, we'd have to show. It was clinical, these examinations, the same anywhere you went. We didn't even mind them, not especially. There was a way they made you disappear. As if every time we lifted up our shirts when we were asked to, we became less ourselves and more just only an expression of our disease. The fruiting of a larger thing. Like the way a mushroom is just a tiny piece of some other, bigger body underneath the ground.

But when we got to Golden Apples, Lee told us he could look at us and see more than just the numbers or what was written in our charts. He said he could look at us and see us as we were. With him, morning check-in wasn't about the scale or about peering at the patches on our skin. His exams were different. Sometimes for example he would have us stand in front of him and repeat a phrase or words. Or he would have us hold very still or he would ask us to move our arms in a certain way or bend our neck or turn our head. And he would sit in his chair in the little exam room while we did this, and he would watch us and take us in.

His gaze was special, like an examination, like a kind of touch.

The moon cut behind the branches of an apple tree and cast us into shadow. In the sudden blackness, Hesper tripped and fell against the side of the house. And we thought it was done, that it was over, that he'd been waiting for us, that he'd found us and the tears started right up in our eyes. We froze together and braced ourselves for what would happen next but in the end we were alone. In the end it was just the two of us and Hesper had only tripped over a tree root and there was no one waiting in the shadows there to grab us and take us back. We hugged each other underneath the window and huffed out a quiet laugh and felt silly about the way our vision had clouded over when she fell. How for a moment we had caught the honey and olive oil scent that lingered on Lee's skin, how for a moment it had felt like every piece of the air around us had been made from his searching, pale blue eyes.

Girls' Choir

(girls are always) in the garden

We were hiding from Lee down by the river, looking at the ants that were crawling along the bank and dipping our fingers in the cold water and trying not to laugh. Eleni moved a leaf and found two slugs crawling over the opened body of a third. After a while we saw they were eating it. Except for the hole in the dead one, except for the gentle spill of guts, it was hard to tell the dead slug from the two living ones. Hesper said she kept losing track of which was which but Eleni said it didn't matter. We watched them for a long time, but then our feet went numb and the ants were biting the backs of our legs and we began to wonder if hiding was still fun. If we were still having a good time.

Is this fun? Hesper asked Eleni, but Eleni just shook her head and held a finger to her lips. Lee had found us though without us knowing and he reached his long arms out quick from just behind us and picked us up. And we screamed because really, we hadn't known at all that he'd been there. We'd laughed too, feeling him gather us together and we felt our hearts shoot up inside us and we wondered if he'd been able to see us all along. If the way he'd looked for us and called for us had all just been for show, if he'd known from the beginning just where we'd been. If he'd known all along about the place we liked to run to by the river, if he knew too about the ants and the slugs and their soft bodies and them eating each other up.

We'd run away before breakfast, before our morning check-ins. We'd been out in the garden the night before and if we'd let Lee check us, he would have surely seen the dirt between our toes.

Lee was always telling us that he could see us. And sometimes that made us into little children who hid our faces in our hands. And made us say, no you can't and made us giggle right into our fists. And made us think also, can you? Can you really see us always, all the time?

PART II

(seeing and being seen)

three months before the trial

Ari

When Lucy and I spent all day together and then the night, I was afraid she might ask me if I had somewhere else to be. She never did though. Lucy took things as they came. She had her own projects to attend to and when it came to other people, she didn't try to rock the boat.

I had started writing when I spent nights over at her house, taking notes and making copies of the journal I kept for my doctor of all the things I ate. I was trying to tease apart the words maybe or squeeze them until they popped, like I sometimes squeezed soft cookies or those gorgeous little Hostess pies with the iced-sugar tops.

If Lucy got hungry, I'd make her scrambled eggs with sugar on top, then she liked for me to talk to her while she fell asleep. I could lie in my bed and she could lie in hers, she could hear me if I held my face up to the wall. Sometimes she asked me to talk her through a list of diving accidents that she had written out. I suspected that we liked to read them for different reasons. For Lucy, reading out the accidents was about controlling future variables and also about keeping her safe from imagined things to come. I liked to read them though because of how they helped me sometimes to think about the year before.

On those nights that she asked me to read about the accidents, the first that I would say was lost the line. Then we would pause for a moment, tucked up in our beds, each of us thinking of a hand fumbling deep in dark water and the silver flash of a thin line leading up to the boat. Then Lucy would remind us how important it was to keep hold of the diving line when we were deep underwater and then I would say the second accident which was ran out of air. We would wait, imagining, and then Lucy would say this was most likely a technical problem with the dive computers or the tanks.

Next there was equipment failure or sometimes I would skip that one and say oxygen toxicity, and we would think about being poisoned by the gas in our own tanks while Lucy drifted off. Sometimes we talked about getting lost in caves, or other times it was rising tides, or other times it was kicking up dirt and clouding the water until we couldn't see. There was a quiet rhythm to saying out the accidents. It was soothing really. I could see how it put Lucy to sleep.

If the accidents didn't put Lucy to sleep though, she would ask me for a story. Tell me about last year, she'd say. Or she'd say, tell me about Hesper and Eleni. She liked them, or at least the versions of them I told her about. What I told Lucy was that Eleni had sharp little knees and elbows and knew how to have fun and that Hesper had red hair and a nose with a bump at the bridge and that she knew all about animals and apple trees.

Bees would crawl up her arm, I told Lucy once about Hesper, and not ever sting her. Lee kept beehives on the farm, I told her, and Hesper would steal honey from them if Eleni asked her to. Hesper could get us huge pieces of honeycomb, I said. And we would hide down by the river chewing on them while Lee looked for us. He would yell for us, I said. But we wouldn't leave our hiding spot until Eleni said we should. I told her that sometimes we would find bits of bee wing and bee leg in the comb and that Eleni would always eat those pieces first. I told Lucy that Eleni would bite right into them and crunch them up. Lucy always wanted me to tell that bit again, about Eleni eating the tiny black bee legs and crushing all the pieces of their wings between her teeth.

I told Lucy that the farm I had worked on was close to the ocean and sometimes we would wake up at night and smell the salt. All through the summer, I said, until I left in September, I watched the apples grow fat and golden in the sun.

And Lucy said, golden? not believing it. But it was true. Golden apples, I told her. Bigger than my fist. Not like any apples you've ever seen before, I said. I told her that sometimes Eleni would get us out of bed and we would sneak into the garden at night to touch the apples. And they would still be hot, I said. Not warm, I told her, hot.

What did they taste like? Lucy asked, but I said we weren't supposed to eat them. I told Lucy we were allowed to eat anything we wanted in the garden. The fat carrots, the huge tomatoes dangling in bright, multi-colored clusters, the beans that overtook their trellis in a thousand surging vines. The raspberries that were sweet all the way through to the center, the tiny blueberries that grew wild by the river and the tart ground cherries playing peekaboo in their little hanging husks. Anything we wanted, I told her, was ours to eat. But not the apples, I said. We weren't allowed to eat those.

But didn't you ever taste just one? Lucy said. Didn't Eleni? Eleni would have bit one, Lucy said.

I switched to the dog then because Lucy liked the dog and because I didn't want to talk anymore about the apples. He liked to lick our ankles, I said, with his fat, pink tongue. He would catch us, I told her, when we were working. When we were balanced up on the ladders, leaning into the trees. Suddenly we'd hear him panting and then this huge wet tongue would slide up our legs. Lucy shuddered. I hate dogs, she said. But I told her this dog was charming. And anyway, I said, he kept away the snakes.

If Lucy still wasn't asleep, I sometimes told her about the braziers. When I first got to the farm, I told her, it was April, so it still got cold some nights. And if Lee thought there would be a frost, he would get us out of bed to light the braziers and we would set them out between the trees in the middle of the night. I told her that Lee kept matches in the front pocket of his flannel shirt and that he could strike them on his teeth like pulling fire straight out of his mouth.

I said that nothing looked real on those nights, not the trees or the house or the apple blossoms. Even us, I said, even we looked unreal and indistinct, translucent almost, not maybe even quite completely there. The long nightgowns Lee had given us hanging down right to our ankles, our hair all loose and tangled, Lee's spare rubber boots enormous on our feet. We looked like something else, I told Lucy, not quite only girls, on those nights. She asked me what it was we looked like but I said I didn't know. Like girls, but not quite girls, I said.

We had to stay out all night, on those nights when we lit the braziers. So that if a wind came and tipped one into the grass someone would be there, ready to stomp out the flames. On those nights we weren't supposed to talk or sit. We were just supposed to stand still and watch, to keep our eyes fixed on all the little fires dotting the blue and liquid dark.

Lee said we wouldn't be tired. You're stronger than you think, he said. And just like that, standing up all night in the garden became a thing that we could do. And we began to see how Lee was right about us, how he knew us, but I didn't tell Lucy that.

It was all the same, the diving accidents and the stories from the garden. I knew somehow it was. When I said there was a dog in the garden who licked our ankles, it was the same as when I said equipment failure. And when I said I went last year out to a farm to take care of some trees, it was the same as when I said drowned. When we talked about divers losing their way two hundred meters down in the water, that was Lee striking matches on his teeth. They were all disasters, each instance held inside it a certain terrible mistake.

The phone was ringing all the time in my house now during the day when my mom was at work. I would have to find a way, I supposed, to talk to the investigators about Lee.

Nothing was ever simple with Lee from the beginning. Nothing was ever just one thing and not the other.

We stood out nights in the garden, not sitting, not sleeping, because he told us we were strong when for so many years we'd been told we weren't. We'd been put in hospitals and hooked up to monitors and given meds. We'd been kept in bed like so many girls before us, but then we got to Lee's, and he told us we were so much more than anyone had guessed. He said that he could see us, that we could do this thing with the braziers and so many other things we hadn't dreamed of yet. And he was right, we did do things we hadn't ever dreamed of there.

After that first night out with the braziers, when it was morning, we found out that we could do it, that Lee had been right. That we hadn't needed to sleep or sit. There was a newness inside of us, something fresh. We'd gone into the house with Lee and he'd fried us fresh eggs in salted butter. And we'd eaten them without a second thought because we were new and not quite really all the way ourselves. Not girls, not quite, not anymore.

The warm yolks and flecked brown butter had slid down from the corners of our mouths and dripped onto our plates and Lee had laughed and called us his animals. He'd cut hunks of bread off a loaf for us and smeared them with jam. We'd eaten that too and grinned like monsters, like we were who Lee said we were maybe. Like we were filled with possibility, brimming with potential that he could see. That was part of the trick, wasn't it? Almost from the beginning, we needed him to be right.

Once the phone rang late in the evening and my mom had answered it and put me on. The person had said she'd like to know more about what happened, that they were gathering information for a case. And I said I didn't know anything, apart from what I'd said before to the police. And I heard the keys on the keyboard clicking, but then she'd said, in any case, she'd like to get a few more details. If I could tell her how I came to be out there, she said, maybe we could start with that. I'd said my mom had found Lee on the internet, that he'd come out to my house in his van to pick me up. And she'd asked if that was usual, for girls like me, when we went into treatment. I'd said I wouldn't know. And that had been the end of it and I'd hung up.

My mom found Lee after I'd been sent home from another program. I had been in and out of programs with other girls like me for years. Sometimes my vitals would dip at an appointment, and I would get checked in to the hospital or sent away. I would stay for a while in the new place with some arbitrary collection of similar girls and then I would get sent home and we would see. I would look different when I came home, fatter and with better skin, but I wouldn't be different really, not on the inside. The programs all promised my mom that I would be different, but I wouldn't be.

A nurse told me once that a girl like me couldn't experience herself as an individual. It was textbook, in the literature, she said. She shoved needles in our arms like we couldn't feel it and hooked bags up to our IV's without telling us what she was putting in our veins. If you were in her way, she'd move you aside like those people who work in slaughterhouses move animals or meat. I didn't tell her, but I liked her. I didn't tell her, but I thought she was probably right.

What Mom found on the internet were pictures of a man standing in front of an old California ranch house in Marin. What she found were pictures of apple trees. The blooming promise of a new kind of life. Look at this she told me, calling me into her room, tapping her phone.

It's called Golden Apples, she said scrolling, showing me pictures of Lee and of his garden and his house. Doesn't it look nice? Then just like that, Lee came to get me in his old van with the two apples painted on the door in flaking gold paint. When Lee slid it open for me, he'd said, hop in kid, I don't bite. And he'd had blood on his shirt and when he saw me looking, he'd smiled and said, buddy of mine's been raising a pig. I just came from his house, we've got some great chops for tonight, he'd said.

I don't eat meat, I'd said, which made him laugh and he'd said, don't worry, we'll sort you out. Mom told him to take good care of me and he said he would and then she hugged me, and he pulled the van door shut and she'd gone back in the house. I thought about the other girls like me and I thought about the nurse that told us we were all the same, that until we'd been fed, we were just organisms responding predictably to our own decay. She never asked us questions about how we felt. You wouldn't know, she'd said.

Lee passed me a basket from the front seat filled with dark-purple leaves. Here, he said, bull's blood. Picked it this afternoon. We'll have it tonight with the chops. He had big, capable hands and his blue eyes shone like polished coins and were so pale they drew you closer, just to see if they really were that color all the way through.

Lee took us by the side roads to get to Golden Apples. The scenic route he said, bumping through dusty potholes, driving past farm stands selling this and that. We were almost at the edge of California, driving along the roads that trace those cliffs that are always just about to slide down into the sea.

Lee turned off onto a long dirt road that cut into some grass-covered hills and when the road dipped down into a little hollow, I saw the house I'd seen before in the pictures on my mom's phone. A wooden-shingled bungalow with deep-set windows, half hidden behind the branches of an ancient apple tree.

A brown dog, big like a bear, with matted fur hanging off its back came running. It jumped up and dragged a thick tongue across my window when Lee brought the car to a stop. Instantly, there was something that made me want to hug the dog. Something that made me want to grab him and bury my fingers in the wild hair clumping at his neck. But Lee shouted and leapt out of the car and grabbed the dog and hoisted its huge body right up off the ground in one smooth pull. I gasped and thought that maybe this place was not somewhere that I should be, but then Lee smiled at me through the window, like it was all maybe just for fun. And for a moment I forgot the dog and wondered only if I was supposed to smile back.

The dog started whining and scraping at the ground with its back paws and thick ropes of drool began to slide from its open mouth and down its neck. It all happened so fast. The grabbing, the smiling, the dog's slick, gaping jaws. It all happened before I'd unbuckled myself or even shifted in my seat.

A grey-haired woman came running down the drive flapping a leash above her head. Seeing her, Lee set the dog down. He smiled and waved at the woman and ran his other hand down the dog's heaving back. When she got close, he took the leash from her and clipped it on the dog's collar, patting her shoulder in a friendly way. After they had gone, he slid open the van door and helped me out. Neighbors, Lee said, rolling his too-blue eyes at me and smiling. That dog is always getting away from her, he said.

That was how I met Hercules, I could have said to Lucy. See? He was there from the very beginning, I could have said, but by then Lucy was asleep. So I couldn't tell her more about his dirty fur and the way he would run around the garden at night. The way he would sometimes bark and bark and keep us all awake while he ran wild through the trees, jumping up and snapping at the apples as they grew so heavy in the summer heat.

On Tuesday and Thursday Lucy had swimming lessons at the Berkeley YMCA. I would drive her there in the afternoons and watch her from the deck. Afterwards, we would float up to our necks in the jacuzzi and watch the swimmers tracing out their laps. Boiling away in the chlorinated water, Lucy told me about how when you were diving, you could go so deep underwater that your heart would almost stop, how it would beat more slowly than if you were in a coma. You would still be alive, she said. But in a completely different way.

Lucy told me that when we were diving, the deeper down we went, the faster the surface air would kill us. Even thirty meters down, she said. Even six, and the air up here would be harmful for us to breathe. It would be toxic, was what she said. The oxygen would poison us. Can you imagine it? she said, beaming. Down there, just one breath of this stuff that's all around us would be deadly, would be totally incompatible with life.

When Lucy said this, I missed Hesper and Eleni. I missed them like friends even though we hadn't been really. My favorite nurse would have told you why that was impossible. Why friends wasn't the word for what we'd been.

Maybe we hadn't been friends but we had understood each other. Hesper and Eleni for example would have laughed like I wanted to laugh when Lucy said that about atmosphere. And we could have peeled off our careful faces and cackled and ruffled up our hair and nodded hard with our sharp chins and said yes, yes, yes, toxic atmospheres will kill you. And we could have made dead-eyes and squeezed the life out of air-puffed packets of cookies or bread until they popped, and we could touch the hard and soft crumbs together like we liked to and mash them like we liked to into dust. Because sometimes there was nothing in between the three of us. Because sometimes being sick was sad and also fun. Sometimes it was tight like a hand around your throat and also like a hug from the one who knows you best.

And even though we were maladjusted and had taken therapeutic outings to supermarkets where professionals watched us practice buying things like cheese, that didn't make us wrong about everything. Because Lucy was right and sometimes we were too, we did live in a deadly atmosphere.

Lucy was taking swimming lessons because she couldn't swim. Alison had explained it to me under her breath. We did all the classes when Lucy was little, she said. Her dad and I used to hold her in the water for hours, just walking back and forth in the shallow end and letting her kick. But she never got the hang of it, and now this diving thing, Alison sighed, shaking her head. The YMCA offered an introductory diving class, but to do it, Lucy would have to be able to swim a lap in the pool all by herself.

In the hot tub Lucy told me the way that diving sometimes made people forget. It's a common phenomenon, she said. They forget things they knew up on the surface, like the names of animals or plants. But also, they forget sometimes the things that happen to them down below the water when they come back up. They'll come out of the water and the dive will all just be a blank. Only sometimes, when they go back down, when they get deep again, they remember all at once. Why can't we ever just talk about how we might see some pretty fish? I asked her, teasing, and pushing her a little with my shoulder into the jet.

Lucy knew why she was taking the lessons. She knew the diving course was coming up and she knew about the lap that she would have to swim to take the class. She didn't bring it up though and I didn't either. I just took her on Tuesdays and Thursdays and when it was time for her to take the test, Alison drove us both.

I'd thought somehow that she could do it. That when it came down to it, Lucy would figure it out. In the end though, Alison and I only watched her pick one foot up off the bottom of the pool and then the other, and then we watched her rotate slowly around, drifting on the tips of her toes. I wanted to tell Alison maybe that was better, maybe that way Lucy had of turning leaden and not doing a thing she didn't want to was better than passing a test. Alison knew it anyway though, without me having to say. She looks like a dancer, like almost graceful, Alison said, grinning and watching Lucy spin.

In the car, driving home, Lucy said that I should take the class. You go and I'll watch, she said, to see how you get on. Pool work isn't really my kind of thing anyway.

Too artificial, not at all like the real thing. I'll be interested though to hear what you think though. Then she leaned into me and said, please do it Ari. And so of course, I said I would.

It was nice when I went to take the class with Lucy. It was fun. Beside the pool, waiting for the class to start, Lucy hugged me and told me that when we were really diving, when we got down deep enough, we would shrink to half the size we were now up on the surface. I wonder if that means we'll be able to slip into places we wouldn't be able to get to up above, she said. Like little holes and cracks in the rocks. I wonder if that's part of the fun of it, the getting smaller and smaller as you go down. If that means you can go to more and more secret places the deeper down you get.

We waited by ourselves for a while, until eventually the instructor came out of the locker room. There were supposed to be other people, he said, zipping up his wetsuit, but they called to say they couldn't make it. Anyway, he said, I guess it's just us.

Lucy helped me into my wetsuit. When I was in it, she hugged me and zipped me up. I could feel the way she lined the wetsuit zipper up exactly with my spine. And this made me smile because that was just what she was like. Tell me about how it is. How it really is, she said, hugging me and stepping back.

The instructor spit into his mask and told me to spit in mine. Rub it around on the inside, he said, or the glass will fog. Once I had the mask spit-cleaned and pulled tightly on around my face, he had me sit down beside the pool with my legs dangling in the water. He brought me a vest with a tank on the back of it and he showed me the hoses and the mouthpiece and how I should breathe. It will feel heavy when you go down in the water, he said. You'll be surprised by the weight. Out of the corner of my eye I could see Lucy leaning toward us, taking in everything he said.

All you're going to do today is try to find your balance underwater, he told me, holding up a tube attached to the diving vest. See these buttons? One is to go up, and one is to go down. You only push them very gently, he said. Try to balance, you're looking for the place underwater where you're not going up or down. The place where you're only hanging, where you're not moving at all. You'll know it when you feel it, he said. You'll be pushing the buttons and bobbing up and down. And then you'll get it. You'll feel it like a hook in your back.

When we're underwater, I'm going to ask you lots of times if you're OK. Like this, he said, making an O between his index finger and thumb. If you are OK, he said, you make the same sign back. Otherwise, I'll bring you up.

I pulled some fins onto my feet and he cinched me into the vest. I hadn't thought really of what it would be like to go into the water with so much weight strapped to me. How it would feel sinking below the surface and maybe not being able to get myself back up. He made the OK sign and I did too, and then he pushed me off the side and into the water and a hole opened up in the surface and I went through it and then I wasn't there. Up above me, the surface rippled and then lay itself out over the top of me as flat as glass. I saw Lucy's blurred face and then I didn't because I was gone and somewhere else.

Lee wanted me to wash my hands before dinner. He said so in the kitchen that first night at his house. Hesper and Eleni were already at the table. Lee had called them my sisters when he'd introduced us. He'd laughed when I looked surprised and said that we were all family in his house.

When I didn't get up from the table right away to wash my hands, Hesper stiffened and Eleni told me that I should do what he said. They both wore identical white dresses that covered them from their ankles to their wrists. From their seats at the table they both watched me carefully, their eyes flicking, taking me in.

Duck fat popped and spluttered in a pan on the stove and Lee lifted one of the chops to check the darkening crust. He crushed sprigs of thyme in his palm and threw them in a pot filled with steaming new potatoes. Relax Eleni, he said without turning around. Give her time. When she's ready, she'll go.

The kitchen windows looked out on a pool, its dark water choked with algae and overhung by the branches of surrounding trees. At the edge of the pool, deck chairs lay haphazardly, resting on their feet or on their sides or on their backs like beetles. Roots pushed up everywhere, cracking the concrete of the patio and snaking down over the sides of the pool. So many roots that the ground outside the kitchen windows twisted with them, so many that it almost gave me vertigo to look. From the windows, looking over the pool and the trees and the garden beyond, it was like the whole house was sitting on a writhing nest.

Lee told me the rules while he cooked dinner. I was going to eat what he served me. All of it at every meal. Or he'd have Jess, the resident nurse's assistant, shove a feeding tube down my throat. Hesper and Eleni watched me and grinned, because sometimes we weren't comrades. Sometimes we were solitary animals ravenous for punishment. Sometimes we were hungry to receive it and sometimes we were dying to watch it get doled out. I got up to wash my hands and Lee took a nectarine from a wooden bowl and cut it into wet, jeweled dice.

He hadn't needed to tell me that anyway, about the tube. Or explain about how he would take away my cell phone and go through my bags. The rules at these places were all the same. With girls like me, treatment programs liked to keep things simple. Girls like us were black and white thinkers people told us. We relied on rigidity. What we needed most was a firm hand. Anyway, I was used to rules, rules were something girls like me understood.

I washed my hands and went back to the table and Lee set down a chop in front of me all crisp and golden in its crust. A white rib curved right up out of it, like the animal had had handles inside it instead of bones, like its living muscles had always just been meat. A pile of torn lettuce lay in a bowl on the table, slicked with oil and shining with vinegar and salt. Take some bread, Lee told me, passing the basket and I took some. Put some butter on it, he said, passing me the plate.

The sun dropped, and we three girls watched each other at the table. Stabbing things and cutting things and putting them inside us and mashing them all up into a paste. I'll push you to your limits here, he told us, but it will make you better. It will be for your own good.

He taught us butchery as a way for us to learn about the healing power of touch. To do it right, you have to really understand the body, he told us, running his knife down the body of a plucked chicken and opening it up. We would have to come back to our bodies he said, slipping the knife in between the pieces of the chicken and portioning it out. We'd have to be inside ourselves, specifically, he said, we'd have to find our own muscles, our own tendons, our own meat and veins and seams.

When he was done, the chicken lay out all in pieces, all glistening, all blush colors and perfectly arranged. We could see inside all the folds and layers and we were hungry then to see what had been hidden, to see it all and bring it out into the light. We took in all of it, the slippery blue veins, the white tendons, the bright slicks of green. We touched it all when Lee said that we could touch it. We ran our fingers over the soft muscles, and we slipped them beneath the pimpled skin. We rubbed and twisted at the bones and pushed and poked at the smooth membranes that stretched between the ribs. We smiled at each other with our slicked fingers, there was so much to be touching and to touch.

Healing touch, Lee said, is about integrating the injured pieces of the body, to bring all the pieces together back into the whole. You can't take up residence inside yourselves until you've built yourselves back from the beginning. Right now, you're like this chicken, he told us, just a bunch of separated parts.

Later when we ate the chicken, we touched its cooked bones with our tongues and let the garlic-laced muscles of its legs fall apart inside our mouths. Later, when we killed the chickens ourselves and cut them up, we thought about Lee and what he had said. How a body could be healed with the right sort of touch. Maybe healing was about being taken down into the right sort of pieces. Maybe that was what we were supposed to understand. We weren't sure, we weren't supposed to ask questions. We were just supposed to listen and watch.

That first night after we had eaten, Eleni and Hesper picked up their empty plates and put them right up to their faces and licked them until they were clean. I watched them and Lee watched them and then Lee turned to me. In the half-darkness his pale blue eyes looked like they had other, even paler, even bluer eyes behind them. I picked up my plate too and licked it while Lee and Hesper and Eleni watched. After I had finished, Lee collected our plates and stacked them neatly in the sink and said that we should go to bed. Upstairs, when we had brushed our teeth together and were tucked in our beds, Hesper and me in one room, and Eleni in the room next door, Lee came up and wished us goodnight. I fell asleep looking out the window, watching the black branches of the apple trees scrape against the sides of the house.

Swimmers' legs kicked furiously up above us, clouding the surface as people fought for air. Underneath though it was absolutely still and quiet, all just one bright wash of chlorinated blue. The deep end was deeper than I realized and when my knees scraped the tiled floor, the surface seemed very far away. I was heavier than I'd accounted for and so much bigger and I was cinched very tightly in my vest. When I hit the bottom of the pool it felt like I would push down through the tiles, right through the band-aids and hair ties that littered the pool floor.

The instructor sank down beside me and fiddled with the buttons until I rose a little off the floor. We took a couple laps around the bottom, moving slowly like manatees, huge and fat, unhurried and majestic. After a while, I found it, that place where I wasn't rising or falling but was only moving very slowly through the water, parallel to the floor. It was different than I thought it would be and I was different than I thought I would be too. Calm I guess, is what I was, tranquil, barely moving at all.

Lee ran a group session every morning after breakfast, where we would perch on the chairs in the living room and listen to him talk. Sometimes he would have us do activities, things like lying down on the floor and closing our eyes and holding hands. Once he had us go out into the garden and eat grapes. He said that we should eat them until we didn't feel full. He said he would tell us when to stop. And we pushed handfuls of them one by one down inside us while he told us how we were always holding ourselves back. Only now we wouldn't, he said, because he wouldn't let us. Only now we would be free. And we ate until we couldn't feel the muscles in our faces chewing, until the juice ran down our necks and pooled in between our fingers and soaked the collars of our dresses. We ate until we weren't girls anymore but just thin skins stretched tight over juice and pulp, waiting for him to tell us to stop.

Before I was ready. Before I could say wait, I'm not done. Wait, there's something else, there's something to pull out from down here, something I could use or take away or bring back, the instructor brought me up to the surface and I was cold and wet and heavy and surrounded by the hectic pool noise. My eyes were shot through with chlorine and I found that I was shivering too much to undo the buckles on my vest.

Leaving the locker room, we passed the dive instructor and he waved to Lucy and called her over. Hey, he said to her, come over here. He told Lucy that he could see that she was a real diver, that he could see that the pool just wasn't her thing. He said he knew a secret place, a beach, where there was a cave that you could get to at low tide. You guys should check it out, he said, winking at me and pressing a piece of paper with the name of a beach written on it into her hand.

two months before the trial

Eleni

It was the morning of the professor's party. Mitch was cooking already, and the smell of meat and roasting bones was flooding up the stairs. I rolled myself up in the sheets and let the warm cloud of it envelop me, the caramelizing onions, the wine reducing on the stove. Later, when I went down to the kitchen, Mitch had coffee keeping warm for me in the pot.

I poured myself a mug and spooned sugar into it until it turned all thick and syrupy and I thought about the way termites use the big mounds they build like external guts. Or, how fungus slips itself inside the thing it wants to eat and not the other way around. How it's not obvious, how it's not necessarily right, the way we operate. The way we do things like we do. It's so solitary, so demanding, the way we mash food up inside our mouths and swallow it, how we digest throughout the day all alone and by ourselves.

I spooned more sugar in the mug until the coffee wasn't coffee anymore but soft like sand. Until it was an ooze that would grind away your teeth. I thought about a line of termites spitting wood pulp all together into a fungus that would digest it for them. How they organized the tunnels of their mound to move the air, to breathe for them together so they wouldn't have to even breathe alone. I peeled an orange and left it all in little pieces on the counter, digging my fingernails into the rind and squeezing the pulp into wads and chunks and bits. Mitch asked if I could peel some apples for him but I said I'd promised Nic I'd help her practice for her class. I left the coffee and the sugar and the peeled rind and the orange bits on the counter, the juice pooling and sticking in the grout.

Nic always needed someone to practice on. She was six months into a degree at the massage school and four months into a program for her cosmetology license. I could have told her when I'd moved in that I liked massages but she hadn't asked. She could just see that about me I guessed, the way I liked being touched.

She was always working on new techniques. One week it would be something to do with relaxing sounds and she would start by hitting a brass bowl with a little wooden stick. Another week it would be about different kinds of oils and another she would be covering my back in hot stones. Sometimes she would be working on deep tissue massage and she would dig her elbows into me and I would try to breathe like she told me to and stay relaxed.

At first I thought she might have wanted my opinion on what she was doing, on if something was hurting or how it felt. But she liked it quiet, she said it helped her concentrate. Besides, she said, her teacher told them to listen to their client's skin. Nic told me that meant I didn't need to talk. I tried hard to be an adequate stand-in for all the other bodies she would go on to move and push and touch. Sometimes though it was hard to keep quiet. Sometimes I felt individual and I wanted to ask her if she saw something special or different when she was working on me. When she was pushing into my shoulder or rubbing my calf or tracing lines down the side of my face.

Her fingers were always cold. So cold that it was like she kept bowls of ice somehow near her and was secretly plunging her hands in and freezing them through. I didn't mind though. Sometimes after her massages I'd get bruises but at the time I'd be so numb I wouldn't feel a thing. With Mitch I sometimes had to concentrate on not feeling, but with Nic the not-feeling came naturally. I wondered if that meant anything or if all kinds of nothing were the same.

Down in the basement Nic was sleeping on the massage table she kept in her room, but when I came down the stairs she jumped up. She swept the pillows and blankets and candy wrappers off the table and rubbed her eyes and said I could get undressed. There was a script that they learned at school about undressing that was supposed to make it unremarkable, that was supposed to make the client feel at ease. I had never minded getting undressed though. I wanted to be like a termite sometimes, dragging my soft abdomen through tunnels that could eat my food for me, my body just one of many others that were all exactly the same as mine. I kicked my clothes into a pile next to Nic's pillow and wrapped myself in the towel she kept hanging on the back of her door for me.

Right, she said, dimming the light. I've got to practice this for class. She had me lay on my stomach and she put her hands on either side of my hips and started rocking me. It's this new thing we're learning at school, she said. We pull you up and then we watch the way you fall back on the table. It's supposed to inform our choices during the rest of the massage.

Termites would all fall the same way, I wanted to tell her. With termites, there wouldn't be choices or watching or decisions, their bodies would all behave the same. But by then Nic had gone quiet, and I left her to concentrate on lifting me up and letting me fall back down.

Lee had told us that we were special, and he told us that he could see the ways that we were different and remarkable too. He said he would have seen that about us, that we were exceptional, even from a mile away. He always told us that he could see all the way through us. All the way to the bottom of what made us tick. Which was maybe why I was down in the basement with Nic in the first place. Maybe I wanted to ask her if there was something that he'd maybe missed. It could have been anything, a mole, or a hair in the wrong place or a vein on my leg that stuck out. I wanted to see if she could see something that he hadn't. Something about me that he'd gotten a little bit wrong, or at least not all the way right.

Nic finished lifting and dropping me and reached a hand up between my shoulder blades and began digging around under the bones. With her other hand she pulled a large carrot out of her pocket and bit off the top. She liked to keep carrots in her pockets, during massages she was always pulling them out and taking bites. Sometimes she had celery, or sometimes she popped pearl onions in her mouth. Mostly it was carrots though. She ate so many that her fingers glowed a little orange at the tips.

Sometimes she would press down so hard that sweat would stand out on my back. I didn't mind it, it felt somehow productive. Like she might be getting down to something. Like she might find something there if she just flattened me out. I wanted her to dig her nails into me like I ripped apart the oranges but that was never the assignment she was working on.

Lee's eyes had been the first thing that I'd noticed when he'd come to get me. There was something in them that could pull you close to him, just to feel them sweeping over you, just to see them right up close. He could pull you in quick too with his tan farmer's arms. He'd reach out sometimes and grab you or pick you up. The thing was though, you almost couldn't tell the difference, between when he was looking at you and when he was pulling you close and picking you up. That was what his eyes were like. How much they would take you in. I'd been at his house a long time and now I wasn't. Now it was just me alone and not all of us girls and him together, and that was good sometimes but sometimes not.

When we left Lee's house, we said we wouldn't talk about it. We said maybe anyway there wasn't anything to talk about. Maybe nothing had happened really. Maybe it had just been another treatment program and maybe we'd just finished it and we'd move on to something else. I'd left other treatment programs though and it hadn't been like this. Me all hollowed out and missing things, me bereft.

The police had come to Lee's house, and there had been questions. Then they'd taken us down to the station and there had been more. We'd said it was an accident, what happened. That Lee didn't mean it. That anyway it was fine and that we were fine too. We'd said no, no, no, it wasn't like that. That it wasn't what they thought. At the time, the police had only nodded and written down our information. Then they'd called our families and told them to come and pick us up.

Hello, there's been an incident, the police officer said when he called our families. Holding hands and sitting on the bench at the station, we weren't sure which incident the police officer had meant. And we'd wished terribly that Lee was there with us, so he could tell us if the things that we had said were right.

We'd gone back to Lee's house after leaving the station but Lee hadn't been there. We'd walked through the empty rooms together and collected our things. I looked for him in the kitchen and beside the pool and out in the garden but I didn't find him. Then we'd said bye, see you, to each other and gotten into our different cars and driven away.

Termite colonies can live for more than a thousand years in the same mound. Then one day they'll abandon it and it's not clear why. One day they'll all just leave this enormous place that has taken care of them for generations. This home that has been breathing for them and digesting their food. I wondered if sometimes they went back to visit once they left or if they never did, and if they never did go back, I wondered why. Maybe they couldn't have run away twice.

Sometimes I thought about the room I'd slept in off the kitchen in Lee's house, and the little bed I'd pushed up against the wall. Sometimes I thought about the apples glittering on their branches and the way it felt to twist them off their stems. Sometimes I thought about it and then I thought, but maybe it was nothing. Maybe none of it had been the way I'd thought.

Sometimes Nic would wrap my head up in a towel, twisting it tight and pulling it right down over my eyes. Then I could drift and be just a standard, practice body. Then I could think about nothing for a long time. Sometimes after a massage she would wash my hair or cut it or sometimes she would paint my nails. This time though she only ran the back of her cold fingers lightly down my face and blew a kiss from the door and said she had to get to class.

Later in the polished dining room of the professor's house, arranging stacks of napkins for the party, I could still feel her hands on me. Like she was with me or like I was still with her, or like I wasn't there except for where she touched me, just broken-up scraps of skin.

Mitch was arranging trays of cheese on the professor's dining room table, interlacing them with sugar-coated walnuts, pots of mostarda, and Marcona almonds roasted with fresh thyme and salt. I wanted to run my hands through the almonds and lick my salty fingers and pinch the soft cheeses like they were cheeks. I remembered spreading fresh ricotta on thick slices of bread at Lee's and lying under the shade of the apple trees in the hot afternoons. I remembered how natural it had seemed there, to do that.

Don't forget to tell them I'm opening my own place, Mitch said when he looked up and saw me leaning close to all the food he had arranged. Then Katy came in and asked if I could bring out a round of drinks. We're just through there, she said, pointing down a hall lined with plants.

I found the students clustered in little groups, talking in hushed voices in a high-ceilinged room. There were folding chairs arranged in a circle around a fireplace and windows overlooking a balcony soaked in late afternoon light. Everything was warm and ready for thoughtful conversation. I liked the weddings better, where I could just be a body in among the other bodies. Not a whole body even, just a pair of hands with a tray. Here, the students were so quiet. They didn't look up when I came in. They didn't cheer or reach for drinks. The glasses on my tray started to wobble, chattering and tinkling and swaying at the base. Not like at weddings where my hands were always steady as rocks.

In the big room, there was only the rustling of my steps on the high-piled rug. No dancing, no clamor, no other people swinging their arms and talking in loud voices and taking up space. So there was room for other things to come creeping, those dogs in their cages, the squeak of metal doors swinging open on their hinges. Maybe there was something that was keeping them inside, something they loved about being locked up. If it was quiet enough and if I wasn't busy, sometimes I thought about that.

On my tray, the bubbles streamed and fizzed out into nothing. I really needed the students to take the Prosecco I was offering, so I could rush back to the kitchen and get more and bring back more for them to drink and eat. But they wouldn't take the glasses. At least not nearly fast enough.

A man in a rumpled blazer moved to the center of the room and welcomed the students. I walked towards him to offer him a drink. Instead of taking a glass, he looked past me and held up his hands and all the students sat down at once. Then it was only me and the professor left standing in the middle of the room. Me and the professor and all my lonely glasses of Prosecco, flat and warm and full up to their useless, sloshing brims.

The professor smiled at me kindly and the students smiled at me kindly too. They waited for me to leave. They were all so impeccably polite. As I backed away from the professor, a glass tumbled off my tray onto the floor at a students' feet. Everyone watched as she rushed to pick it up. Sorry, she whispered, putting the glass back on my tray. She held the glass so lightly, almost not even touching it. It made me miss the weddings, everyone here was so terribly self-contained.

When I got to the edge of the circle, the professor clapped his hands together and the students settled back in their chairs. Now, the professor said, what shall we make of all this? How shall we begin to untangle things this evening? He smiled and asked the students which one of them wanted to start. He seemed like a good teacher, like someone who was careful and who took his time. Someone who could really help explain things when they got hard to understand.

I stood behind the chairs for a moment, watching him and watching the students too. Some of them had pens poised already above their papers, ready for any excuse to take notes. One of them raised a hand and said something about focusing their research on gaps in the archive, the silences in the original texts. There was a question I didn't catch, then another student raised his hand and said something else. I stepped back into the shadow of the hallway, balanced the tray in one hand, selected a glass and drank.

Mitch had tried to match the menu to the evening. He was obsessive about things like that. Details, the why behind a filling or a topping or a sauce. He would be in the kitchen finishing the canapés – sliced duck breast stuffed with apples, set on golden discs of fried brioche. There were small glasses of dry cider I was supposed to take around directly after. It was all supposed to come out in a certain order and be a certain way. It was supposed to be appreciated just so and bit by bit.

Mitch would be caramelizing the duck in the kitchen with his torch. The edges would be crisping, turning just a little black. The professor said something about Hesiod, about maidens in a garden. He said, now what can we make of….? but I was already too far down the hallway to hear.

I dumped the rest of the Prosecco in the plants so Mitch wouldn't think I'd done a bad job passing out drinks. When I got to the kitchen with the empty glasses, he asked me what had taken so long. I said they'd started talking, that maybe we should hold off until they were hungry, but he said the duck couldn't wait. He gave me the tray of canapés and told me to take it out. The duck slices lay so sleepily on the brioche, so deeply soft and red, crisp just at the edges and slicked with just a lick of sauce. Mitch told me to hurry. Hurry, he said, that duck is dying on the plate.

Voices drifted toward me down the hallway, people talking about myths and girls. Katy was in the classics department. She'd had to tell me what that meant. Greek stuff, she'd said. Roman stuff too. History, language, culture. Oh, I'd said, like gods and heroes. Yeah, she'd said, more or less.

I walked behind the students, sauce dripping off the edges of the duck. The smell was unbelievable, butter and salt, apples and blood. I wanted so badly for them all to want it. For them to turn around and see me and to reach for me like they reached for me at weddings. To call me over and take all the things I had. But they only bent deeper over their papers and no one turned around to look.

One of the students was talking about Hercules, that name I recognized at least. He said that he had written a paper on the Hesperides in love. The professor clapped and said that he remembered that one. Excellent research, very retro, the professor said laughing, which made half the students laugh and the other half take faster notes. I took another turn or two around the room, tracing out a neat half-circle behind the chairs.

The sauce was clotting and the duck had started to congeal. Where before everything had been glistening, slick and crisp and hot, now the fat was clouding, smearing into grease and the sauce was breaking into gruesome lumps. Someone had pushed a coffee table up against the bookshelves in the back of the room. I left the tray there and went back to Mitch.

He had a tray of cocktails waiting. Hurry, he said. They've got to have it right after the duck. Tell them it's called the Golden Apple. Make sure you tell them I'm going to serve it at my place. I took the tray and headed back to the students, dipping my chin down and sipping one of the cocktails as I went. It was bright with lemon and apple juice, vodka and Calvados. I took another drink. It was good, but it wasn't right. That's not what it was like, I wanted to say.

I leaned against the wall at the back of the room and crushed an ice cube between my teeth. I listened to a student talk about a paper she had written, something about girls in stories doubling as gifts. All the students kept their hands busy writing or adjusting their glasses or hooking their hair behind their ears. They were all leaning towards the professor who was nodding and inviting the student who was speaking up to the front of the room. The cocktails gleamed all together on my tray.

The student got to the center of the circle. She was very small and I almost couldn't see her over the other students in their chairs. I picked up another drink and sipped it. She told the others something and they nodded but I didn't strain to hear. Instead, I listened to the ice clink against the side of the glass. A student in a green sweater asked about the dragon. He said, what about the dragon? How did the dragon figure into things, he wanted to know.

When she finished and there was clapping while she made her way back to her seat, I darted up to the student who'd asked about the dragon. I tried to offer him a cocktail, but he was too busy taking notes. What did he mean about the dragon, I wanted to ask him. I wanted to tug on the sleeves of his green sweater and ask him what he thought the dragon meant.

In the end I dumped the rest of the cocktails into the houseplants in the hallway and went back to the kitchen to find Mitch. What is taking so long, he said, spooning black swooshes of tapenade onto a tray of hot cheese tuiles. I thought about telling him that the students weren't really eating, but he had already given me the tray and a bottle of wine and was waving me out. I dropped the wine into some of the houseplants I hadn't watered yet and set the tuiles next to the duck. The poor duck and the poor perfect tuiles were languishing. No one was eating. I couldn't help them though, there was nothing to be done.

I went back and forth for a while between the students and the coffee table, the trashcans and the kitchen and the plants. I was trying to spread it all out. Someone raised her hand and said, don't we use mythology to tell the stories we can't talk about directly? But the other students only said yes obviously, and she blushed and wouldn't say anything else.

When I left the kitchen with a bottle of chilled Gamay and a tray of honeyed dates and found the students still absorbed in their discussions, the trashcans full, and the plants all listing in their pots, I walked the other way down the hallway and found a door that let me out. Behind the house a sprawling garden climbed steeply up a hill, unspooling above me out into the dark. I followed a gravel path through some trimmed hedges, pinching dates off my tray and squeezing them between my fingers until they popped.

A curving set of mossy steps led further up the hill, I dropped the dates behind me, leaving a trail of sticky, pulpy bodies in my wake. When I got tired of climbing, I crumpled myself up beneath a tree and sat with my back to the house. I'd thrown the serving tray into a fountain somewhere down below me but the wine was still cool when I put the bottle to my lips.

More than one of the students had brought up the golden apples, but none of them had speculated as to the taste. None of them had wondered if they were bitter or if they were delicious or if they were sweet. None of them had asked what it might have been like to steal one from a tree. It seemed like, for all their talk, they were missing the point. None of them had asked about the project of tending apples that weren't ever meant for eating. Some of the students had talked about the Hesperides, but none of them had asked what sort of girls would be good at doing that.

None of them had asked what it might have been like to watch those golden apples hanging on their branches and want them and not want them all the time. They didn't ask why Hera picked those girls particularly. What had made the Hesperides particularly perfect for the task.

My hands were covered in honey, I shoved them in the dirt so I wouldn't be tempted to lick them and then I drank the rest of the wine. I closed my eyes and waited for nothing or for everything, I wasn't sure.

Eventually some ants found the sugar on my fingers and I felt them come streaming up my arms. I let them cover me and make a shape out of me in the dark. It was wrong what we did at Lee's house, but so was everything that I was doing now. I was trying hard, but I wasn't getting it right. Why hadn't the students wanted anything, why had I been left so terribly alone. I wondered if the evening would have been different if only one of them had taken something from my tray.

The next morning there was another letter taped to the door of Mitch's house, it was from a lawyer looking to get in touch. Lawyers and other sorts of people from the state had gotten involved with the case at Golden Apples. They had questions that they wanted answers to, but they didn't seem to understand that I didn't have any answers to give. The police, the lawyers, the people asking questions sometimes said, it's ok, you can tell us. We already know, they told me, we just want you to tell us what you saw. When they said that, I wanted to ask them that if they knew what had happened, if maybe they could please tell me what it was.

seven hours and forty minutes before the trial

Ari

I pulled Hesper up and she winced and reached for the leg that she had twisted on the root. I put her arm around my shoulder, and we leaned against the side of the house. We held our breath for another minute, but it was quiet still and no one came for us. And I thought maybe that would be it. Maybe Eleni would come out and we'd go back to the hotel and the next day at the trial we'd say the things we were supposed to say.

I thought maybe it could all be over, that we could go home. But then the smell of olive oil came towards us and spices toasting in a dry pan. If we held our breath, we could almost hear the rattle of them as they scraped and rolled in the heat. Hesper said, he's roasting grapes. And I could smell them too and we knew the dark turn their skin would take as they blistered in the oven, rolling over and over in the bubbling wine. We knew the way he cooked them, the way the grapes would swell. The way the char would bloom out all thick and black across them in the pan.

Grapes roasted in red wine had always been Eleni's favorite and sometimes when she'd run away and was hiding in the garden, Lee would cook them to bring her back. Smelling the grapes now, we remembered those nights when Eleni had been hiding and we knew just what Lee meant by making them for us. And we were suddenly so sorry for the way we had behaved, and we thought maybe we'd been wrong to ever leave. We felt too all very keenly the way we'd been so desperate, so ravenous, for all the months we'd been away.

Hesper was saying something, but I hadn't heard it. I'd left her without my knowing it and lurched towards the back of the house. There was a kind of heat coming towards me, drawing me closer and folding me up. I'd only just now seen that I'd been waiting for it. Waiting and waiting for it for the better part of a year, waiting for it while I ate all that peanut butter and almond butter, those measured tablespoons of butter and sour cream.

Hesper caught me then, stumbling, saying we should call a cab, saying we should get that taxi man to come and take us back. He could do it, she was saying. He could come right down here all the way into the garden, he could come right now and take us back. There was no service in Lee's valley though and we both knew it. And anyway, neither one of us had our phones. Then I was pushing her away and walking towards the kitchen with the back door that was always propped open for us. Because I could smell the grapes ballooning in the heat, their skins pulled so tight around them, about to burst. I could smell the way they were almost ready, the way they would be slick and black and bubbling in their juice.

I let Hesper's voice fall away off me. I let it drift off into nothing as I edged around the pool, the dark water still all scummed and slick with algae, all that green revolting growth. I told myself that if Hesper was quiet now it was just that she was better, that her leg had untwisted itself off somewhere in the shadows around the side of the house. That now I didn't hear her because she had left, because she was back already maybe in her bed at the hotel.

And as the thought of Hesper became distant, it became harder and harder to think about her at all. Harder too to think about the road and the taxi that had brought us here, it all seemed so far away. The garden had a way of making nothing else outside it real, of erasing things or making you forget.

Light spilled out from the kitchen windows, flooding towards me by the pool, making the room glow like a lantern in the dark. It made sense. The glowing, the light of it, the way it was the only thing. The kitchen had always been at the center of everything that happened there. Lee, standing with his back to us, cooking at the stove. Lee wiping down the counters or whipping frosting for a cake. Washing the dishes or oiling his cast iron pan or butchering meat. It had all taken up so much of our attention the year before. So much of our time had been spent in that place.

Eleni was sitting in her chair. She had made herself small against the table, almost leaning into it, just like she used to do the year before. I could feel it, the way she had one leg wrapped around the other, the way her foot was pressing hard into her calf. I could feel the sweat pricking underneath her arms and creeping into the fibers of her shirt and the way she was drawn tight like a cord. I could feel too the way that she was buzzing. The way she was relieved and ashamed and disgusted and overjoyed to be back.

She was reaching her hand down into Lee's glass and picking ice out of his drink and putting the pieces in her mouth and cracking them between her teeth. Lee was at the stove, flipping something in a pan and bending down to check on a sauce. She was drumming her fingers on the table and it was so quiet in the garden that I could hear it, the little beats her fingers made against the oiled wood. A wind blew lightly through the garden and the apples tinkled in the branches of the trees.

Lee pulled the grapes out of the oven, I could smell them even where I was outside. Then he looked up, right at me standing by the pool and he grinned at me through the glass. I thought I would have been afraid to have him see me, but what hit me then was just absolute relief. And I would have gone right in and sat beside Eleni and waited with her at the table for the grapes, except that just behind me then there was a crack. A branch snapping back against the house, and I turned away from the window then and I saw her. Not Hesper standing right behind me, but another girl.

one month before the trial

Hesper

When I left the apartment and went running out to catch the bus to work, I passed Dave on his porch, smoking and pick-picking at his beard. He was so deeply digging and so much twisting his fingers into the hair and into the soft and pale skin underneath, that my face lit up all along in the same places where he was touching his, and I could feel my stomach do that deep little catch and flip. The dry scratch of his fingernail against all that spongy under-beard skin was so blue and rich like the way a river is cool and flows so freshly past, and makes you want to dive down to get to that pale skin too. I couldn't help but lean listening right into it, swaying in the build and the release of it, in all the flaking dead skin cells flying off just everywhere and flashing out like little sparks.

Somebody came by looking for you earlier, he said taking a step back from me leaning raptly into him and his beard and his gorgeous rasping scratch. And I quickly rearranged my face and tried not to be so much looking at him scratching and tried also not to be so much with my own fingers clenched and with my eyes so wide and watching that they gave me all away. I tried not to see the way his fingers paused and started twisting at something that was caught or stuck or swollen near the corner of his mouth. Same guy's been coming around a lot, Dave said, still digging. He says you never answer your door. I could feel the scab lifting off underneath his fingernail, the dry crust of it just inching off his face. He says he's got something for you that's real important. Any idea who this guy is?

He took his finger out and flicked the picked bit away and I flew with it for a moment, just all out and tight and open, and then I was back in front of Dave. Now that he had finished scratching, I was piecing it together, what he'd said about the someone coming round looking for me. And I squeezed my face right up like I was thinking, but not of much or anyone specific.

There was a sick feeling inside me though. I was too afraid to ask if the person who was knocking at my door had blue eyes like when full sunlight hits flat water and makes you stagger and see only white. Or if the person who was coming round had long, tan arms and big hands and a head of thick white hair all out and bristling just like a mane that you wanted to sink your fingers in and touch. I thought maybe he did, that the man who was looking for me might have had those things. But then again, that man wouldn't have had to knock. That man would have known when I was home and he wouldn't have talked to Dave. He would have walked on his long legs up to my door and called my name, and when he called, I would have opened it right up. I made my face all soft and fine like a cat's back and I told Dave I didn't know who it was. I told him that I didn't have any idea who could be looking for me.

By the time I was on the bus, my fingers were already moving down the line of my jaw, stretching the skin and feeling for ingrown hairs and bumps. They were only just innocent, my fingers, only just brushing against a couple little spots. Just flicking. Just feeling the way they bulged, the little bumps, the scattered spots. The way they were slightly hot.

Nothing really happened anyway, I said to myself. Nothing that would make him come looking for me. I ran two fingers down from behind my ear and underneath my chin and pushed my head down and to the side until I heard a crack. The trick was to do this all very slowly, so I wasn't really doing it. To just have it be something that was happening to me. Anyway, it wasn't me, I said. I had just been there. I hadn't done anything at all. When there were three stops left, I told myself that I could use my nails, and not just the pads of my fingers. That for three stops I could run them lightly down the sides of my face. I crossed my legs one way and then the other and told myself that Dave was wrong, that no one was out there looking for me. The bus hit some traffic after three-stops-to-go, but I was already using my nails, and the scratches would start any second to show, so I had to get off at an earlier stop.

I could hear Lee rummaging around inside my bag, rolling an apple over and sniffing it. This apple's not organic, he said. It will fill you all up with poisons that will stay forever in your fingernails and teeth and hair and rot you from the inside out. I said I didn't have time to talk to him right then, but he only scoffed.

He kicked the apple down inside my purse and said that I was backsliding, that he'd have never stood for it. That an apple wasn't lunch. What about some grilled lamb, he said. What about the bloody little shreds of it? Then he smiled and said, remember the way I used to cook the chops? I said thanks but that I'd find something later, which made him cackle and roll right over on his scaly back. You're not going to, he said. You're just going to eat the apple and then you're going to throw it up. You shouldn't be walking around, he said. A sick girl like you. I see what you're doing, he said. I know what you're like.

You know who's looking for you, he said, the words all tumbling out from behind his clacking teeth. You know just what this is all about. Stop pretending that you don't. Then he jumped out of my purse and flap-flapped away.

The library was quiet, so I sat at the reference desk and mostly looked into space. At 13:13, I took my lunch. I grabbed my bag with the apple still inside it and walked up the stairs to the third-floor bathroom which was the one I liked. I wanted to keep Lee away, so I walked with my head held steady on my shoulders and made my thoughts blank and white and loud. Like a huge storm where I couldn't hear any one thing.

It didn't matter though; Lee was waiting for me anyway on the stairs and he was laughing and even with the whole ocean roaring, I could still hear his voice. He was laughing so hard that he was rolling on his back about it, and he was giggling and picking over all the details with his sharp little claws. Shoo, I said, using the firm voice that I practiced sometimes in the mirror.

He'd never really cared about whether I was standing up to him though. He just curled his dry scales around my neck and slipped down the top of my sweater and slid once around my chest and down the length of my back. I told him I didn't care. That he wasn't real, that he was only in my head. He twined himself then tight around my arm for just a second, gripping me fast, squeezing me and wringing a sudden sweat out of my skin, then he wriggled down to my wrist and jumped off into the air.

You're not there, I told him. Not really. No one else can even see you. You can see me, he said. I checked my wrists for where the marks from his claws would have been, while he preened his feathers up above me in the window. I waved my arm at him and said, see? There's nothing there. He only picked the window open though with his sharp little teeth and lurched out and was gone.

I thought about running up the last steps and throwing the apple out after him but I was afraid it might hit someone who was really there when it came down. So I just sat on the bench in front of the window where he'd been preening and started picking the apple apart. I twisted the stem off and sucked on it and ground it up between my teeth and started pinching off bits of peel and flicking all the juicy little pieces down into the trash.

Lee was coming around and finding me every day now. He wasn't leaving me alone, he was pestering me at work and he was going through my fridge at night. He watched me sometimes on the bus, or when I was in the supermarket, rolling my hands over all the best fruit. He watched me walk over to the frozen yogurt shop on Telegraph at midnight and order the extra-large fat-free, sugar-free cup, and he peeked at me in the Costco food court where I sometimes went to watch people stuffing themselves, folding huge slices of cheese pizza down into their mouths and face.

In Costco, he would look at me the same way I would look at the people that were eating. Which was like my eyes could erase just all the space between us and there could be nothing at all between my mouth and theirs. Sometimes, lots of times, someone would order two slices of pizza. And I would watch them heap the slices, one after another, past their gaping lips. And I would swallow when they swallowed, all curled up on the hard plastic bench seat, sipping at my ice-water and crossing my legs tight and taking with them bite after bite. Sometimes a long string of bubbled-brown cheese would come telescoping frantically out of their mouth. And I would feel it pulling too so soft and greasy at my lips. And I would feel just desperately warm and full-up then, watching all those slices disappear, seeing all those slick mollusk tongues shove the cheese-packed slices down the backs of all those throats.

Lee was always watching me at Costco, even though he knew I didn't like anyone to see me there. At Costco people could see what a messy, greedy person I was if they looked. Sometimes, he would perch on top of one of the food court umbrellas and click his tongue at me or sometimes he would curl up underneath my shirt and nip at my bra straps while I chewed on ice, or sometimes he would trace circles around my ribs.

He would slither up between my shoulders and tisk his disapproval when I bought jars of sauerkraut and mustard at the gas station and ate them with packets of Sweet'n Low, stirred in until it looked like yellow sand. Or when I drank liters of Diet Coke in the shower, or when I lay in the bath and picked my scabs until they swelled a little and turned the water that cooked-salmon color, that Thousand-Island-sauce pink.

Lee said he was coming around because I was slipping. Because I was scratching and picking and skipping meals and acting sick. But also, I noticed that he was shedding scales when he slithered up my sleeves and that sometimes he wore a pinched look. I couldn't ask him though, about whether there was something wrong. Or why he was showing up so much after all these months. I couldn't risk the question because you never knew what Lee would do. Sometimes he would be funny and surprising but other times he could be mean.

Once, in the garden, he'd picked Eleni up and thrown her in the pool and she'd hit the water so hard that there had been a crack. She had pushed up out of the water laughing, but she'd had her hand pressed to the side of her face. She'd waved at us with her other hand and smiled through her fingers though, and then she'd flipped over and done a backstroke through the algae and the slime. Later, snuggled up between the two of us in bed, she said she'd known that he was going to do it. That she'd known before he threw her that he was going to pick her up. I wanted him to do it, she said. And it was marvelous, she told us, twisting a bit of my hair in her fingers. I just felt weightless, when he threw me it felt like I could fly.

I didn't think so though. I didn't think Eleni liked it. I didn't think so because of her face. Because of the way it was just before it hit the water. Sometimes I felt the same, that electricity, that blankness like a flash that whites everything out. Maybe she didn't remember what her face had been like, or how she'd been saying no, no, no, before he picked her up. Maybe Eleni didn't remember that.

Lee had been mad about something when he'd thrown her. We'd gotten something wrong, or at least we'd gotten something not quite all the way right. He'd lashed out and then her feet were up off the ground, and she was tumbling out above the water. There had been the slap, the crack of her when she hit, and then Lee had smiled when she came up out of the algae holding her face.

Lee had shrugged, like it was all just for fun, and he'd crinkled his eyes at us and asked Ari and me if we wanted him to throw us in too. Ari shook her head though and said she'd get in on her own and she jumped in and ducked her head underneath the algae and then I'd jumped in too and we'd all dragged our feet along the slimy bottom and pushed up out of the water and laughed. Then Lee had turned and gone in the house. Sometimes it was like that, like we had to guess.

Later, we said we were sorry for jumping in, for not trusting him to throw us and I'd thought maybe that I should have let him scoop me up. And I wanted to cling to him fiercely and tell him I didn't want to miss my chance. We'll do better next time, Ari said.

We should have been better about it, we shouldn't have been startled or caught unawares. It wasn't out of character after all, Lee throwing Eleni in. He loved surprises and he liked to play games. It was therapeutic, he said. It was good if we couldn't know all the time what would happen next. And he was right, I was always reaching out so hotly for control and wrapping it up so tightly right around me like it could keep me safe. It's not keeping you safe, he said, holding my fingers for me, holding my hands for a minute in his.

So they were really for the good. His games and surprises. They were part of what we needed to get back to living in the world. Don't worry, Lee told me, when he saw I was worried. It's all part of the plan.

Sometimes he would wake us up at night, and he would have baked a cake and he would have us play games like Simon Says, or Red Light, Green Light. Games like we might have played when we were little, but always the kind where we had to pay attention to him, games where the game was to do what he said. If we made a mistake playing, we had to take bites of the cake.

Once it was a chocolate cake with whipped cream and cherries soaked in whisky. We gaped at the way it towered on the plate. At all its soft layers almost toppling, at the dark curls of chocolate and the way they just so lightly tumbled down the sides. At the gleaming cherries, at the way they were almost winking at us in the candlelight, all just reclined and dozing lazily in the fat and sugar and cream. Another night it was cheesecake with a tangerine curd, and another it was white chocolate with raspberries and a hazelnut ganache. He never cut slices, only set the cake out on the same green plate with a single spoon stuck in the top. And when he caught one of us not freezing when we were supposed to freeze or not moving when we were supposed to move, he'd come over smiling and tag us, sliding the spoon across the width of our palm.

Later when we talked about the games together, as we were polishing the apples up in the trees or dipping our feet in the water down by the riverbank, we would open our eyes up so wide and say that it was awful! The nights with the cakes and the games. One of us would say we couldn't believe we'd had to eat it! And the other two of us would nod. Still, when we were talking, we would all remember that spoon sliding across us, of the way we'd all really deeply down wanted to be made to do it, to take those bites.

You girls are losing like you're asking for it, Lee would say sometimes, crinkling his eyes at us and tapping the back of the spoon against his teeth. And we would scream a little and say, never! And we would promise really truly that we weren't. That we were all absolutely trying our very best to follow all the rules and to be the best good sorts of girls. But our hair would be matted with sweet lemon curd, or there would be crumbs around our lips, or we would have dark streaks of jam running down the sides of our faces.

We would be wild and funny and so much fun on those nights when we were playing. We could be amusing, very-charming girls. We could be a lark, because finally we had someone we could trust. We could finally sidle up right next to all the things we'd ever wanted because we had someone who was strong enough to pick us up and hold us back. We could run straight at those things so freely, and we could laugh at them and take enormous bites. We could eat anything, really anything, as long as Lee was there to tell us when to stop.

When the game was over, Lee would take the spoon and put it in the sink and we would get cleaned up and tuck ourselves beneath the covers in our beds. Then we would go to sleep like it had all been nothing or had never happened, like it had only been a dream. Sometimes it all felt like that there in his house and in the garden, like there was a white heat spreading over everything and we were just all dazed and fat and blinking in it.

Blink, and we would be up on long white ladders polishing the apples with skin-soft cloth. Blink again and we'd be sitting at Lee's table, falling like dogs on steaming new potatoes or crisp radishes dipped in salted butter, or a golden roasted duck. Or blink and Eleni would be slapping down into the pool. Or we'd be in the house at midnight and Lee would just have said red light and we would have frozen so fast and quickly in our skins trying to hold every piece of us so still while Lee watched us to see if there would be a loser, clicking that long spoon against his teeth.

Lee said I wasn't doing well without him. He knew that I was eating my lunch in the bathroom now, and he watched me in my apartment at night rolled up in blankets, eating tubs of Diet Cool Whip underneath my sheets. He'd watch me flailing and he'd say he'd known I would struggle, and he'd come sliding along in between the spots where I'd picked my skin and lick them with his little dragon tongue and remind me that he knew me best. I know you're there, I'd say, when he was there. But he said I didn't always know.

I left the library and went to get iced coffee from the cart I liked outside. I had started by getting just one coffee from the cart but now I always ordered three. Lee would cackle if he was there to see me, and he would flap around and watch me peel the tops off the cups and spill packet after packet of Splenda in and swirl and mash them up all deep into the ice.

Someone tapped my shoulder while I was stirring and asked if I was Hesper and I said yes. Then a man who wasn't Lee put a letter in my hands and said I had been served. And I fumbled with the coffees and knocked one over as I opened up the letter and found my name printed out all in black and white right next to Lee's. The letter said that there would be a trial and I was wanted as a witness. I tried to call after the man to ask him what it was that the state of California thought I might have been a witness to, but he was gone.

seven hours and thirty minutes before the trial

Ari

The girl behind me was wearing one of those white dresses, the same as I had worn at Lee's the year before. And the fabric of the dress was oh so bright and dazzling that it was like it had been cut straight out of the darkness all around her with a knife. And I saw then how it was, how the girl inside that brightness was a piece of violence and how inside that violence, she was lost. How she was simmered down, and all reduced to sharpness. How she was just abandoned to it, that wanting, those ravenous bones.

It seemed there had been some breeze, some sudden gust, and that the dress had billowed out just all at once around her because it was unfurled and wide and tangled like a sail in the spreading branches of an apple tree. And it seemed almost that the tree was grasping at her and I thought I maybe saw them weave and twist themselves down like vines into her hair.

And I wondered if I was about to get very loud. I could feel a yell just welling up inside me as this girl who looked so much like the girl that I had been started to pick and pull herself now out of the clinging tree. And I could feel the bark splintering beneath her fingers, and I wasn't sure if I was still and quiet, or if really, I was running up the drive. Or if I was in the house and ripping down the curtains in the kitchen or tearing the sheets from off the beds.

The girl had been trying to slip her way out gently but then something seemed to startle her, and she started to twist and yank at her dress. And as she pulled and twisted, the apples up higher in the branches began to knock against each other, sending up that yeasty musk that I'd forgotten all about while I'd been gone. It caught me like a plough just underneath my ribs and snatched away my breath and I sagged a little and thought, I'm not ready to remember this.

The girl was pulling hard now at the fabric, but there was so much of it all ratted and tangled up in the branches of the tree. And I thought maybe she was like a spider and was just spinning the dress right out of her like silk. And she was all joints and bones and staring eyes and didn't look quite like a girl at all but something horrible, something else, just caught and turning this way and that way in the tree.

I couldn't see Hesper. I hoped she'd run right back up the drive. I hope you're gone! I wanted to yell to her, and I wanted her to be far too far away to hear. There was a ripping sound and the bottom of the dress tore right off and the girl came away wrapped just up in the shreds of it, tumbling out of the tree. She put an arm out and caught herself on my shoulder and where she touched me, I could feel how deadly cold she was. The apples shook and that scent was rising out of them, that rot and ripeness, like they were green and hard and young behind their golden armor but also soft and rotten too and dripping all inside with awful juice.

Now that she was near me, I could see that I was so much warmer and so much bigger than she was. I had eaten so many peanut butter and almond butter sandwiches since I'd last been in the garden but there was so much of me that still remembered what it had been like to be like her. I wanted to reach up and grab the apples and tear them down off all the branches but also, I wanted desperately for them not to fall.

Finally, the apples settled back onto their stems and the girl turned to me and I saw there was a white haze glazing over her pupils, like a fog had come and settled in the center of her eyes. And she looked so much like Eleni, and so much like Hesper, and so much like me, standing there in the garden like she was then, in her torn white dress. Of course, I thought, of course there would always be hungry girls in this garden. Of course, there would have been other girls that had come after we had left.

Through the window, I could see the real Eleni tear the end off a fresh loaf of bread. She held it steaming right up to her nose and inhaled and then she dipped it down into the pan of roasted grapes. And I could see even through the window, the way she pressed it hard into the juices and it was so much like so many other nights the year before that I wondered if maybe I had never left.

The garden was closing right around me, I could feel the tightness of it nipping so friendly and familiar right around my chest. I wondered if time could get just stuck, repeating sometimes in pockets. I wondered if this other girl was really Hesper, or if this other girl was me. There was a jolt, and the ground beneath us tilted and the girl grabbed me around the waist with her cold arms as the trees began to shake.

PART III

what we wanted (apples)

Girls' Choir

in the garden (keeping secrets)

We were eating too many apples and we knew it. We're eating too many apples, we whispered, giggling into each other's soft ears. We said it chewing on the white flesh of apples and we said it splitting the bitter, golden seeds of them between our teeth. We're eating too many apples, we said. But we were always reaching up into the branches for another one, grinning as we plucked them from between the leaves. We're eating too many apples, we murmured to each other from beneath the covers, our red, raw fingers always itching for the next stem's wet snap.

Our bellies were turning hard and tight like early-summer melons. They were swelling neatly, all prim and identical, like a new kind of crop. And we who had been little twiggy girls for so long, who had hated and been afraid of the treacherous expanse of skin beneath our shirts, were beside ourselves with ravenous delight. We're like little drums! we said, pounding on our swollen tummies. And we could beat out a bright little thrumming tune on them, taking turns or all together or one or the other one of us drumming on the rest. And our gums were raw and rawer from all the sweetness, and our tongues were becoming just as red as candied fruit. And we laughed and curved our backs and admired ourselves in the bathroom. And we pinched our cheeks and said that we were getting good and fat.

At night it was hard to sleep because we heard the apples tinkling in the branches, and we heard them calling to us all the time. And sometimes we went out alone to eat the apples after Lee had visited us. And sometimes we went in pairs, when one of us was otherwise engaged and sometimes we went out into the garden all three of us together to eat and sleep and play. That way it didn't matter really what was happening to any single one of us, because the rest of us would be out in the garden eating apples, snapping them freshly off their stems and stretching our jaws wide open and taking the most enormous bites.

Lots of nights we sighed hard and said, thank goodness. Thank goodness we're just little drums. Thank goodness we don't have to worry anymore about being girls. It had been so hard when we were girls, was what we said.

It was only that sometimes in the mornings, when our sheets were stained with apples, when we woke up all smeared with the traces of that golden skin, that our bellies felt sometimes like girl's bellies, and then they hurt us and were sore and we ached with them and for them and near them and in them and they weren't drums or melons anymore for just a moment but were us, and we were just so desperate then and so tired and scared and full.

four weeks before the trial

Ari

We'd driven out to the ocean, to the parking lot near Point Reyes the scuba boy had recommended, but we hadn't found the secret place he'd told Lucy about. We spent the day picking our way around tide pools and peeking in at anemones and cold little fish. At low tide we walked out towards the water, and I ate my snack while Lucy looked for the entrance to the scuba boy's cave, but there was nothing like what he had described. No rocks cutting out into the water with arches in them to duck under, no secret lakes. Only slate gray water and cold wind blowing sand into our faces and coating our cheeks with salt.

When we got back to the car we ate our sandwiches and I told Lucy I was sorry about the cave. That should have been the end of it, except that as we were throwing our wrappers into the garbage, Lucy spotted a path cutting down into the high grass. I knew I should have said that it was late, that the tide was coming in, that it would be getting dark, but I didn't. I didn't because I wanted to find the secret beach too and because I wanted to be a cave diver and not writing in my journal about sandwiches and because I wanted Lucy to be right.

We left the car and walked down behind the dumpsters and let the grass hush and rustle right around our shoulders as we started down the path. And I felt a coolness then, a certain drop in pressure, like we were landing in an airplane or going somewhere down quite deep. Lucy must have felt it too, that dropping feeling, because she turned back to me and smiled, and the grass closed right up behind us and hid us from the parking lot.

The path passed through a stand of coastal pines and opened onto a rocky promontory that cut straight into the water just like the scuba boy had said. Lucy pointed to a darker place down on the beach below us, a break in the face of the cliff. That's it, she said. The tide was coming in but Lucy wasn't looking at the water. She had her eyes on the crack in the rocks. Then, in an instant, she was moving, scrambling down the rocks to the beach.

He said there's a way in through the rocks, Lucy told me in the car when we'd been driving out. He said it's hard to see from up above, but there's a place in the cliff down by the water where we can get in. He told me that we'll have to crouch down really low at first, like almost crawling but he said that it would open up and then we'd see it, the big cave and the lake. And I hadn't turned the car around or stopped but only just said that it sounded quite amazing. Like just the sort of secret thing that she would like. But now the wind had picked up and I was supposed to be in charge and there was all that cold water creeping up the beach.

Lucy was already down on the sand. I thought that I could let her go and follow slowly, that she'd wait for me or come back. But she ran all the way down the beach and I saw her stop at the dark place and duck down and then I saw her disappear.

Just like that, she was gone, and time went heavy all around me, like it had sometimes the year before. The way, in the garden, it would sometimes stop.

The police had asked what happened when they'd come out to the garden the year before and found us and things and how they were and now there were lawyers asking the same questions all over again. Just gathering information, they said when they called me on the phone. Just tying up loose ends. But the only thing that I could ever think to say even now, even still, was that sometimes the air was heavy in the garden and that sometimes, time stood still and let things happen that couldn't be accounted for. But that didn't help to answer any of the questions that they asked.

The lawyers wanted specifics. Details they could write down on a piece of paper. Facts. But what I wanted to tell someone was that sometimes it was so warm and humid in the garden that the air was like a body hanging on me and that sometimes the minutes pooled right around me just like blood. I mean the way it clots sometimes inside you and the way sometimes it spurts too fast and flows. Too fast, and things would happen quick, quick, quick. Too slow, and one minute would just refuse to tick over and become the next. It was like that on the beach when Lucy was there and then she wasn't. All quick and slow and paused just in a deadly way. I could see her there ducking down and then I couldn't see her, and I could only see the place where she had been.

No one had asked me, not the police, not the lawyers, about what it felt like. But I wanted to tell someone that time in the garden was sometimes like a hitched-up breath. I mean sometimes, in an instant it would all go quieter than quiet and so still that I could hear the apples twisting on their stems. And sometimes all the minutes would come unhooked from one another and I wouldn't be able to tell if something had happened before or after something else.

And I wanted to tell someone that then, when everything came just undone, there would be Lee smiling at us in his kitchen. And there would be Lee sliding pink sausages into a sizzling pan. And also, there would be his fingers in the dead meat of them, stuffing them into their slippery cases the day before. And also, there would be Lee saying he did it because he loved us. And also, there would be his hands tracing just such light circles on our shoulders and there would be him saying loosen up. And also, there would be us laughing and feeling all fed and fat and full-bellied and losing the dry tissue-paper look of our skin.

Lee said once that we were powerful. That we weren't just sick girls but girls with something to give. What if you could give it? he asked us. What if we were special? What if in our sickness, we were a kind of beautiful gift?

Lee said it again one night when he was splitting plums at the table, the fruits laid out all bare and rocking gently on their backs. That day there had been a fight between him and Jess. She had yelled at him and then she had come and found us upstairs. I'm leaving, she'd told us. You need to come with me, she'd said. But we hadn't gone with her and then Lee had been at the bottom of the stairs. Not saying anything, just standing there watching and then Jess had left. We could hear Jess waiting for us in the driveway with her car running and we peeked out the window and Hesper pulled down hard on her hair and asked us if Jess was right. Is something wrong here? she said.

And I said no, and I said there was nothing wrong. I said that we should stay because we were getting well. We heard Jess drive away and out of the little valley and Eleni and Hesper were nodding and listening to me. Nothing's wrong, I said. If it feels wrong, that's just because we're getting better. Didn't getting better always feel terrifying? I said. Didn't it always feel dangerous? Like walking out on ice? And we curled back up on the bed together and then it was just us and Lee in the house. And we pinched the little bits of fat that had grown across our bellies, and we felt the way that the skin there had grown a little soft.

And we were getting better. And we were warming up. And we were like the lily pads that lay drifting on their backs down in the pool, we were opening and opening and growing in the garden and just soaking in all that late summer light. And if it felt wrong, that was just us, just the way we were. That was just the kind of sickness that we had.

After Jess left, the house went quiet. It was August, and the heat crept into the house. We were less like patients with Jess gone. We stopped morning check-ins because she wasn't there to take down our blood pressure and note our weight. We didn't stop getting better though. We were eating at the table then more and more like normal girls. And Lee said that we were beautiful. And he would say it when he was salting a roast or rubbing a vinaigrette into delicate green leaves. We loved to hear it. That we were special, that we were gorgeous, that we were getting better and better all the time. And that was one of the things that I hadn't been able to tell the police. That we could have left. That Jess would have taken us. That she told us to leave. That we didn't listen. That it was my fault.

I got down on the beach and my chest pulled tight like it had been snapped with a rubber band. I knew that feeling, that leg buckle, the sudden pull right down to the ground. I put two fingers quick up to my neck just underneath my jaw and pressed hard to check my pulse. Then the beach blinked out and instead there was Eleni creeping up the stairs at Lee's. And then there was the sound the garden made sometimes at night, like the apples all had little golden hearts, all drumming out the same low pulse inside their shining skins. And I lay there on the beach and let it all wash down over me because I had memories tucked up inside me that weren't at all like memories but were like things happening over and over again.

I was in my bed and Eleni came so quiet up the stairs to our room and shook me and Hesper by the shoulders.

And we said that we were tired, that we wanted to sleep, but she only shook us harder and pinched us with her cold fingers and pulled our hair until we were awake. Then she said we had to come meet her in the garden. And there was something so hard in her then, like her eyes had swung loose from the rest of her and they were black and chipped and glinting like little stones. She slapped our cheeks to be sure we wouldn't go back to sleep. Then she left and we followed her because we always did, picking our way down the stairs, bruises blooming lightly blue just on our shoulders from where she'd pinched us, our cheeks red from the back of her hand.

We found Eleni by the pool, and we saw then that her nightgown was torn down to her waist. She only smiled her wide grin though and told us to follow her, to run and just before we got down to the river, Eleni stopped and pulled us up into a tree. Crouching then like birds up in the branches, she took our hands in her hands and wrapped our fingers all together around a little golden fruit. There was a kind of shiver then that passed through us and through the garden and then we pulled down hard and the apple came away into our hands.

Picked, it was soft and warm and so thin-skinned, like a plum. Like the way they're just so heavy sometimes with all that juice. I was the first one to bite it and then I held it up to Hesper's lips and that was how we all came to eat the apples even though we knew that was the one thing we were supposed to never do at Lee's house. We tasted every part of the apple, the skin of it and the meat of it and the little golden seeds that popped and fizzed in our mouths when we split them with our teeth.

Eleni wrenched another apple from the branches and we ate that one quickly too, and bits of skin and seed got all caught between our teeth like little golden stars winking in the black holes of our mouths. And there was such a smell then in the garden, such a rising sweetness. And when we bit the apple, there was this rush of juice. Our skin flushed red where the apple touched it, around our mouths and in long lines where the juice ran down our necks. And we laughed and picked more apples and burst their golden skin between our teeth.

Eleni spit an apple core into the river, then she twisted off another and set it whole between her teeth. Hesper and I saw then how her nightgown was really ripped to pieces, how it was tied together at the shoulders and lay open at her hips. We blinked and asked Eleni what had happened. But she didn't answer and in the quiet her eyes were only two black pools, just swimming in the paleness of her face.

There was a burning, a kind of building heat and I tried to spit out the apple I was eating because it was turning all to acid in my mouth. There was something wrong with Eleni. Something in her face that I had missed. Beside me, Hesper started to pull her hair as we watched Eleni wrench the last apple off the tree.

Then Hesper gasped and said, Ari, can you feel it? And I said yes because I could feel what Hesper meant. Because sometimes we were all of us just like a single person. And we could feel the hands that had been crawling up Eleni's skin. And we felt how cool she had been when he had touched her. How very still. How just exactly like a statue in a fountain. Those cold, stone girls with their blank eyes and round lips that let the water run over and over every part of them and never moved an inch.

Eleni's head lolled and she toppled back against the branches all lumped and disarticulate and tied up only loosely in the pieces of her dress. And I tried to grab her then and hold her and put her back together and make her real again and like Eleni but the tree, gone all ashen and stripped of apples, shuddered then and cracked. And we fell beneath the ruined branches to the ground.

The place in the rock that Lucy had gone through was smaller than I had expected. I wasn't even sure how she had gotten through. I bent low and called out, Lucy! Lucy! Lucy! but she didn't answer back. Then there was nothing left to do but go inside and get her and pull her back.

I got down on my hands and knees and started pushing right into the rock. And I wondered how Lucy had got so small because I had to move one shoulder forward and pull one back to get inside. And I thought then, squeezing into the little passage that this couldn't be the place the scuba boy had told Lucy about. That this was not a place he could have ever fit.

There was a moment when I almost couldn't fit either. When I had to really push my shoulders in, and my back caught all hunched and awkward on the rocks above. And I felt held suddenly very tightly. When I felt gripped, like I was being stopped. And I thought of all the times before when I had so badly wished for something hard and strong and just immovable to stop me and then of course I thought of Lee, who had. Then the rocks around me eased or I got a little smaller because I tipped right through into the passageway beyond.

My hand fell on something warm and coiled in the sand. I shrieked, but it was only one of Lucy's scarves that must have pulled away from her when she'd gone ahead of me. I bunched it up and stuffed it in my pocket and started crawling forward but I only made it a few feet before I hit my head against a rocky shelf that loomed and crushed the passage into an even smaller place. And I had to make myself even smaller than before to fit, and now the rock was touching every side of me.

Crouched and folded up and crawling, I inched along the passage, sliding right against the rock. My cheek grazed past another one of Lucy's scarves and then there was another and I could see the passage was dotted here and there with things that she had left. I was squeezing through the passage too but only just, like I was a key that had been made to fit. The passage was that small and getting smaller, that tight, that fit to me. Inching on my hands and knees, I would get to where I couldn't move at all, to where I had to crack my shoulders and hunch down just a little more and flatten out my stomach and hold my breath. But then there would be an easing and I would squeeze through until I found myself stuck again. And I would have to find another part of me that I could make a little smaller so I could keep going, keep sliding down to fit.

It felt suddenly so very, very good. Inching myself further and further in, pressing into that place that was too small and then too small again. I thought about Lee. I thought about him because I thought about him all the time. Because he was like the anchor that I towed always right behind me. And I couldn't be just here and trying now to get to Lucy. And I couldn't just be thinking of the tide that was crawling up the beach. Because the rock was holding me so tight just like Lee did sometimes and because there was a terrible relief to it, to being held like that.

There was a place where the rock was swollen, like the passage had some kind of cancerous disease. And I had to arch my back and leave my hips behind me to get around it. And I thought that maybe that was it. That maybe finally it was bad enough, that maybe I could not go on. That maybe I was stuck. But then the sand and gravel underneath my knees gave way and I tumbled out into a cavern and it was wide and vast and marvelous. And I just lay there for a moment on my back and took it in.

The rock arched high up above me. At the top it was cracked wide open to the sky. Light filtered down into the soft and mossy darkness all in bits, shimmering in places and bouncing gently off the sides of the cave. Touching too the remains of other parties, other people who had been this way before. A soft shirt and a knit cap, some crushed beer cans, the top half of a swimsuit, little clusters of half-smoked cigarettes. And tucked into the shadows of the far rock wall, waited the spreading darkness of a lake. And it was perfect. It was just like the scuba boy had promised us.

Lucy was there next to the water, standing with her back to me. Then she kicked her feet out of her shoes and peeled off her sweatshirt and I saw that she had her swimsuit on underneath her clothes. And she looked younger than I'd ever seen her look before. And my heart started to beat hard in my chest because she didn't know anything about caves, not really. And because I didn't know anything either. And because the tide was coming in. We can still get out, I was saying, even though I wasn't sure and the cavern began to echo with the sound of my voice telling her to come back. The echoes died right down around me though as I watched her slip into the lake.

It's fine, she said, after a minute. There's a ledge just underneath the water. And she pulled herself out into the center and floated on her back and the light just caught her and held her and I stopped calling out to her and telling her to stop because I'd never seen her look so very much at ease. It's just like they all said, Lucy whispered. All those divers. All that about those secret caves. It's just as good as they said.

She flipped over on her stomach and pulled herself along the ledge to the far side of the lake until she was deep in the shadows underneath the sloping rock. Come on Ari, she said, her voice echoing and pouring down on me from everywhere, the scuba boy said we could get out this way.

The cave walls were closing in just all around us and I wanted to tell her that I wasn't even certain we were in the place the scuba boy had meant. That the passage we came through had been too small for anyone his size. That if she went under that rock wall, she might never come back up. That there was no way to tell if there was anything but more water on the other side. That above the water, it might only be more rock. That we were both very small animals and not at all real-life explorers. That I really needed her to come back.

I was just sorting through which of these to tell her first, when a sheet of water hit the back of my ankle and I knew it was the tide. The dirty foam of it was then already pouring through the passage, all choked with little rocks and sand and bits of twig. I yelled to Lucy and she turned to look at me. But there was water coming up over the tops of my shoes then and I couldn't think of anything to say.

The branch from the apple tree, all stripped bare and torn at and even gnawed on in places, was pinning us hard down all together on the ground. And we were all so tangled and so closely pressed on top of one another that I couldn't tell the three of us apart. Which elbow belonged to which one of us. Which shoulder, which knee. Which one of us was crying, which other one of us had the black eyes and the torn-down dress. We all seemed so much the same with all our bellies pulled tight and rounded out with apples, with the same golden bits of skin all grimed beneath our fingers and stuck in pieces in our teeth.

One of us was saying that another one of us was dead. And one of us was combing fingers through another one's hair. There was blood too on one of us and one of us was crying. And the apple trees were all so still like curtains, like they would admit no sound to pass them, wreathed as they were then all with deafness and with mist.

It was true that one of us was very still beneath the branch. That one of us had her arms laid out like little twigs beneath us, all brittle and bending at wrong angles right into the ground. And one of us was saying that another one of us was cold. She's so cold, was what one of us said.

And we were all caught then in the garden because the minutes had stopped like they sometimes did. And one of us was going blue and one of us was wiping tears from all our cheeks. She's all blue, one of us said. And we were all beside ourselves and we were breaking up and drifting even while we were lying there together, all stuffed so full of apples on the ground.

In the end it was barking that broke through the heavy stillness and set the minutes ticking and time all back on track. Hercules was coming towards us, bounding through the trees. And he was pushing back the cloying fog that lay thickly all around us. We saw how his fur was wet with it, with all the heavy, clinging mist. There was foam dripping from his mouth and his sides were heaving and when he got to us, he bared his teeth. And he reached his great head down and bit the branch and dragged it off of us and set us free.

We tried to pull Eleni up but we couldn't move her. In the end it was only Hercules who could wake her, blowing hot little puffs of air on her face until she opened her eyes. Then we lifted her and Hercules let us lean her up against him and he seemed to grow bigger and taller as he walked us slowly back to the house.

Once we got inside, Eleni was smiling and she reached up over the stove and pulled down Lee's big pan from its special hook. And we were laughing because she was making her face just like Lee's face. Pulling down her eyebrows at us and pinching up her lips, but suddenly the pan slipped from her fingers and went crashing to the floor. There was a sound then, a rustling and a throwing off of sheets and Lee came into the kitchen all red-eyed and undressed and saw us, and we flew away from ourselves like birds. And also, we were quiet. And also we sat down at our places at the table while he picked up the pan and wiped it clean. He set it on the burner and turned on the gas and we watched the metal of it start to glisten in the heat.

Those apples had made us hungrier than ever. They were burning a hole right through us and I wanted a plate of Lee's eggs to eat. And one of the reasons that we were still there in his house and not back with our families, was because I liked to eat the eggs the way he cooked them. The way he fried them in brown butter and the way he pulled them out of the pan when the yolks were still all raw and wet. We were at his house still because I'd said so – that we were getting better, that we should stay, that we shouldn't go away with Jess.

Which is why I had to snip part of the morning off. The part where when Lee had come into the kitchen, he'd come out of Eleni's room. That the sheets he'd kicked off had been hers. Eleni's flat black eyes from the night before, what Jess had said to us when she was leaving, it all might have come together if I let it. But I was hungry and I was sure that Eleni and Hesper were hungry too, so I got up when he told me to wash my hands and I washed them, and I came back to the table and sat at my spot. I had let people down in my life for so long, but now I was getting better and I was helping Hesper and Eleni get better too.

Lucy saw the tide coming in behind me. So I didn't have to say that it didn't matter anymore, that we couldn't get back through the rocks. The water was creeping towards the lake now and catching her shoes and making them float. And I couldn't remember why I'd brought her here or what we'd hoped to find. I kicked my shoes off beside the lake and watched the dirty water rush over my socks.

Lucy was waving at me from the lake. Crooking her arms at me and beckoning me in. There's another way out, was what she was saying. There's another way through here, just under the rocks. I shook my head and let the tide climb up over my ankles because getting into the lake had to be worse. But there was Lucy waving, and I was supposed to be in charge, and we couldn't get back the way we had come.

I slipped down into the lake. The water was so cold that it made my chest ache. There was rain too, falling in sheets through the crack in the rock up above us and there was thunder and the cave was growing loud with the sound of rushing waves. Lucy was holding on to the rocks at the back of the cave and calling me over almost cheerfully, but I could see the way that she was shivering. How her hands were starting to slip. And I began to feel heavy too with the cold of it and my feet and hands were turning slow and stupid and all to ice.

I wondered if this was two hundred meters down, or if we hadn't got there yet. I wondered if it would have been better if we really had been diving. If it would have been more peaceful, if deep underwater we would have been less afraid. I wondered if the worst of it was when you were still up at the surface, still fighting, with the water filling your mouth and the little waves slapping your face.

On dives, when you were really diving, you went down fast but spent a long time coming up. Going down, you were hurtling, you were making yourself heavy and letting yourself go. Coming up though, you had to be careful. You had to take it slow. Lucy and I had talked about just this sort of thing, lying in our beds and whispering through her bedroom wall. How, on the deepest dives, surfacing could last for hours. How, during those hours you would be doing the right thing by only just lying very still at various pre-calculated depths. How you might float for instance for an hour, or for more than an hour only just a foot or two underwater, breathing the oxygen you had left for yourself at that particular depth. I was so cold, and the tide was lifting me and pushing me into the rock, and the rain was streaming down my face and in my eyes and I wondered if I'd gone down deep enough. If I could start to float, if I could lie very still just underneath a foot or two of water and rest.

Lucy grabbed me by the shoulder. It's just under there she said. And suddenly I could see it, that she was right, that there was a way out through the rocks at the back of the cave. We had spent so much time imagining the darkness, so much time closing our eyes, but we hadn't ever really thought about the light. About what it might be like to see it glistening. Patches of it streaming towards us underwater. Shimmering and there for us to reach.

I'd spent so much time thinking about nine-days-down, about Tartarus, about being cold and small and whittled-down and all alone and slipping through a bottle's neck. But there, just underneath the water was a gap in the rocks big enough for us both. And we didn't have to calculate, or lie very still, or be any other way than just exactly as we were. We only had to wrap our arms around each other quick and kick our legs and dive.

Lucy put her arms around me, and we let ourselves slip down beneath the surface. And it was all soft sand and easy places to hold onto and the way through wasn't even very dark or very deep. In the end it was everything that we had wanted, feeling the way with our fingers, slipping underneath the rocks, pulling ourselves together into all that waiting light. We came up on the other side grinning. And finally, we were divers. We were self-sufficient and indomitable. We were just like Lucy had said. The rain stopped then and the sun caught us and dried our shoulders as we walked back through the water and then the tall grass to the car.

That night when Eleni came and got us was how we started eating apples. And once we started, we never really stopped. Not every night, but lots of nights, one of us or some of us or all of us would slip out into the garden and swim in the overgrown pool and climb up into the trees.

Lee moved Hesper into Jess's old room and we stopped the group sessions that we'd done with him before and we stopped telling him about how we felt. Sometimes it felt like we were living, like we had started life. Hanging out around the pool, swimming, playing games. Living, finally, instead of always only trying to be cured or get well.

I thought about what Lee said all the time. How sometimes he told us all the things we most desperately wanted to hear. You hardly weigh anything at all, was what he said to me, after Jess left, after Hesper moved out, that first night he came into my bed. You hardly weigh anything at all, was what he said. And I was getting better in the garden, and getting better wasn't easy but I was listening and I was thinking about the things he said.

I had told Eleni and Hesper to stay when Jess said that we should leave because at home I had been hungry, and because at home I was always the one who was unwell. And because I was afraid to stay at Lee's alone and because I wanted Hesper and Eleni to be there with me like sisters and because I wanted to keep eating Lee's butter-fried eggs.

At Lee's house, we could have the things we wanted. We could hear that we weighed nothing, that it was easy to pick us right up off the ground. It seemed like there, we could eat bread with butter, smeared thickly and dripping with fresh blackberry jam. That we could eat duck legs cooked slowly in their own rich fat, carrots rolling over in honey-butter glaze, potatoes roasted until they turned gold and cracked, hand-pulled balls of mozzarella, the inside of them sharp and fresh with salt. There, it seemed suddenly all so easy, like we could eat anything at all and also be as thin and fine-veined as a leaf.

Lee cooking for us, treating us like family, like whole and perfect and unsick girls, made it seem like all that might be possible. Like if not quite actually a safe place, it might be a magic one. A place where we might be bright and shining and alive with a kind of perfect gloss. A place where anything was possible and many things might be true and real at once.

I had seen Eleni be the girl inside the fountain on the night we first ate the apples. I had seen her be the statue with the water pouring over her and touching her in every place. I wondered what it was she wanted. What magic she was looking for, what motivated her to make this kind of exchange. I wondered if it was for the hot bread, or the seared lamb, or if it was the short ribs and the way they fell just off their bones or the fresh-picked lettuce or if it was something else. And I was still, and I could be a statue. And when he slipped the nightgown just down off my shoulders, they weren't my shoulders. And when he ran his hands down to my waist, it wasn't mine. Because I could take away my shoulders and make them not my shoulders, and my waist and the place between my legs. But I had been hungry for so long and I wasn't sure anymore that I could take away the way I wanted to eat those eggs.

Girls' Choir

in the garden (hiding and hiding)

We were hiding apples underneath our sheets. Bits of them, clusters of chewed shreds. We were biting off pieces of apple and holding them in our cheeks and sucking the flesh for juice. We were fishing the desiccated remnants out of our mouths and squishing them right all the way down between our sheets to the bottoms of our beds.

We told each other that we shouldn't do it. Can't you stop? we said, shaking each other's shoulders. But we only picked slippery wads of apple skin out from between our teeth and we smiled at each other and said, of course! Look! we said, smiling. We already did it! We stopped just now! we said.

We knew that we weren't being serious. We're not being serious enough! we said. And we pulled each other's hair and pinched the insides of each other's arms. He'll find out about the apples! He'll be so angry! we told each other. And we turned pale and felt a little drop falling down inside us like water going far far far down a well.

He can get so angry, we whispered. And each of us was thinking of some separate thing. He can get very, very angry, we said. And we drew down our eyebrows and we pulled on our most serious face. And we said yes, you're right, we have to stop.

But those golden bits of skin felt so fresh against our feet when we crawled into our beds at night. And we loved to curl our toes around them and feel them sliding up against our ankles while we slept. And when it was dark outside we ran our fingers over our tight little bellies and we whispered to each other, maybe we don't have to stop.

And the trees scratched their branches up against the side of the house and we pulled our rotten-apple-smelling sheets up high over our heads and buried our faces into our musky pillows and said, maybe we don't always have to be so good.

two weeks before the trial

Eleni

It was June and getting warm and the case was going to court. I was bringing around trays of elderflower cocktails at parties and lavender lemonade spiked with gin. Weddings went later and people gave better tips. But all I could think of was the trial, of Hesper and Ari and Lee.

Mitch cooked at night when we got back from the weddings and after he was done he would come up to my room. Sometimes he smelled like vanilla and other times he smelled like roasted bones. I had told him already that I was leaving. There had been Mitch and the parties and there had been Nic, but with the trial coming none of it was enough.

Lee said that we would be able to take care of ourselves when we were ready but that until then he would do it for us. Take over the taking care of us. He said that we were like the apples. That we needed to be up in the branches and close to the tree.

It was June and I had been gone for months and months now and I was missing having roots. I had branches and leaves and all the parts that everyone could see but maybe I hadn't been ready to leave the garden when I did, because it felt like I was missing the part of me that stuck down into the ground.

Now when Mitch called me into the kitchen and said taste this or this, I couldn't taste it. Not his fish stews with fennel and lemon from the neighbor's garden, not his pickled shallots or his roasted tomatoes or his hazelnut vinaigrettes. I was thinking more and more of other things, of honeycomb and apples and of bread. Of potatoes roasted in duck fat and of carrots pulled up by the river and eaten fresh or roasted and soaked in jus. I was hungry and I tried not to be hungry, and I was thinking of blistered grapes.

Nic too was drifting out of focus for me. When I thought about her, she mattered less. When she wrapped the towel tight around my eyes or touched me with her cold fingers, I could only think of those termites streaming out of their enormous mounds. Some of them must go back I thought as she dug into my shoulders or cracked my back or toes or hips. Some of them must be able to go back and live where they had lived before and be just the same as they had been.

The lawyers called me on the phone and asked me questions. They said I had to get my story straight. They said I had to concentrate on what it was that they were asking. Often, they said, that's not what you told us last time. But I couldn't remember what I'd told them the day before. None of it was clear. They asked the same questions and I gave different answers and then I gave different answers again. I had been in Lee's house on the night in question, I had been there, and things had gone wrong. Besides that, I couldn't say.

I got a subpoena with my name on it in neat, official ink. It said my presence was required at the Marin County Court House on June 15th. I got a letter too from the lawyer representing the state. The lawyer wanted to meet with all of us together. He said he wanted to go over certain details. He'd arranged for us to stay at a hotel near the courthouse the night before the trial. He said it would be paid for. What he said in the letter was, the costs would be defrayed. Anyway, he said we had to come.

I turned the letter over and over and I crumpled it up and smoothed it out. I wondered what the lawyer meant by certain details. I wondered if we would say something when we were all together, if this lawyer would ask us better questions than the police.

Things were starting to tighten up around me. I couldn't carry drinks at parties anymore because of the way the trays shook. I was scared of seeing Lee at the trial and I was scared of not seeing him too. I wondered if he had missed me the way that I had been missing him.

Once, on the phone, one of the people asking questions said, look, we're just trying to untangle this mess. Like I should have been more open. Like I should have been grateful to help out. I wanted to tell them some knots are best left tied. And I was so tired, and I wanted to tell them all to go away. I wanted to tell them that I wanted to be polished again and cared for and well-kept.

Anyway, I was packing up my things. The last year had been so terribly hard. And for what? I was tired of passing cocktails and I was tired of parties and of people who didn't understand me, who didn't see me, who couldn't make me real. I was thinking of the garden, and I was thinking I was ready to go back.

seven hours and thirty minutes before the trial

Ari

A branch fell somewhere out in the garden. We couldn't see it, but we could hear the hard way it hit. Beside me the other girl was catching up the pieces of her dress and it was so much like other nights that I had been there and she and I were so much then like other girls. She had those clouds drifting lightly in her pupils, whiting out her eyes and she looked just like I remembered looking the year before.

I wanted to ask her if there was a dog. If it wasn't just that there were girls like us in the garden, but if that part of the story had repeated too. If when she was reaching up and polishing the apples in the afternoons, if there was a dog sometimes that came and licked her ankles. If there was a big dog who ran barking through the garden and woke her up at night. I wanted to ask her if she could scratch his ears for me and tell him that I was sorry and if she could tell him thanks.

Another branch hit the ground beside us and the apple hanging from it split and burst into a pulp. That ripe and rotten smell began to fill the air, like the ground was breathing out their scent. The air hung heavy, charged and tense, as if before a coming storm and all throughout the garden, the apples chimed, shaking and tinkling in the trees.

There was a cry, and Hesper came running, limping heavily on her twisted leg. The apples are falling, she was saying and she was clutching her arm and underneath her fingers there was blood. Inside the house, Eleni had her head resting on the table. And I could feel her, the way that I had sometimes felt her in the garden, like her body was also my body. Like we were braided up together in everything that happened there with Lee. I could feel the way her belly was full for the first time in so long, the way it washed through her, that aching, slow relief.

An apple hurtled down beside me. Then another and another apple buried themselves in the ground right at our feet. We have to get inside, one of us was saying. We have to go inside the house. And one of us was grabbing the other one's arm and one of us was ducking and covering her head. Apples were pounding on one of our ribs and hitting one of us hard in the back and knocking the air right out of all of us at once. Rain broke out, pounding down on the garden and the sound of breaking branches began to echo through the trees. Apples gashed themselves everywhere just so wide open, sinking into the mud and soaking the ground with their inspissated golden juice.

And there was the house with its warm windows and its smell of roasted grapes and baking bread. And there was Lee, watching us through the glass. And when we started running, he opened the door wide and welcomed all of us in.

The air hung soft and expectant in the kitchen, Lee had something for each one of us. Roast potatoes for Hesper, crisp and glistening with oil and salt. For the girl in the torn dress, he'd made carrots. Cut on the bias, set in a prim white dish and swimming in silky glaze. And for me, for me of course there were eggs.

one week before the trial

Hesper

In my bath floating in the oatmeal-smelling water. Bobbing just to and fro all hummingly and peacock blue and like a little rowboat pulling gently through the duck grass all spilling greenly from the shores. I'd dumped a whole bag of oats into the steaming water that morning and now later, later, later the bits of them were all still swirling gently. Like flowers fanning out around me and I felt symphonic and streaming and lush.

It was June and I wasn't really needed in the library since the students had mostly all gone home. I had been taking long baths to help my skin heal and to stop tempting my anxious fingers with all my scratches and scabs and bumps. I was spending a lot of time just soaking and being still. Things were getting slowly better. Like the curved back of a snail. Like I was creeping right along it and going round and round. But the way it spirals I thought, soaking. That kind of shell. Round and round. Going down sometimes and sometimes curling backwards, could all be ways of crawling out.

In the mornings now I took vitamins like I was a scientist. Like I was important, or like I was a special experiment going exactly right. If I didn't take a bath, I took a shower. Then I washed my hair and brushed my teeth. I put on Neosporin and band-aids where I needed to, and I tried to pick less at the spots.

In the kitchen, I was cutting things and peeling things and cooking things and eating things too. Real things like potatoes even. Not just air-puffed things, or sugar-free or diet things, things that tasted sweet all in the same emptied-out way. I bought a blue bowl to eat out of and I was making soups. The days could go well if I skipped light and evenly, like holding your breath. I was getting there and sometimes I could move fast enough to be even breezy. Cavalier too, all jaunty and gamboling.

Lee had been coming around to see me less and less and when he did, he seemed fretful and distracted. Sometimes he held his little dragon head between his talons and covered over his lake-blue dragon eyes and complained of headaches and other times he flew around my head looking miserably off into the distance like he thought someone might come.

At night I'd wake up sometimes and hear him nosing around in my cupboards and I'd shiver and think maybe he'd be all teeth and talons again. All sharp and dangerous, like the way he'd been. But if I crawled out of my blankets and opened up the cupboards, I'd only just find him stumbling and tripping over the cans of chickpeas or the potatoes or the beets. Once I heard him shout and found him tangled in some vine tomatoes and he seemed almost on the point of tears. Curling tight into himself, whining piteously and snapping at his caught foot.

He was shedding hard little scales when he crawled around underneath my sweater, and he didn't come by to watch me cook. I wanted to ask him how he'd roasted those potatoes that I'd liked. How he'd seasoned his stock. He was always only turning in circles underneath my blankets though or crawling up and down my arm and chewing on his tail. His little wings looked dusty, and he was always flicking his tongue, the way a snake does when it sniffs the air. Sometimes I would wake up in the morning and he would be curled around my shoulders. Just drooping and shifting his wings and muttering in his sleep. He would nuzzle deep into my neck if I let him but if I asked him what was wrong he would nip at me and flap away.

It all made me miss furiously some of the things about him. Even the hard things. Even the sharpness of his blue eyes and the way they used to cut me out like cloth. Remember when you grabbed Eleni? I wanted to ask him. Remember how you picked her right up off the ground?

I got out of the bath and showered off the globs of oatmeal where they clumped coldly all together like the wettest little flock of tiny breakfast sheep. All baaing so serenely behind my ears and sulking in the cracks between my toes. Lee wasn't there to watch me take my pills but I took them, even though he wasn't there to see me get it right. Come and see me like this, I wanted to tell him as I mashed up a banana with another banana in my blue bowl with a fork. If you put oats in the bananas and cooked it maybe it could be a pancake I said, and I wished Lee was there to say enough about oats.

I wanted to ask him what he thought about the trial, and I wanted him to laugh about it but also, I wanted him to be afraid. Because I could still feel the way he used to curl right all around me, the way he'd held me and Ari and Eleni so very tight. Because I still remembered how he'd said that the tightness of his arms around us had been on account of how we were, on account of how we needed it. And the complicated truth of how I maybe did. During the trial I would have to stand up and answer questions. But mostly I just wanted to ask Lee if he had been right. Were you right to? I wanted to ask him. Was he right to? I wanted to ask Ari and Eleni too.

Because when we'd been in the garden, or when I had been up in my room and my fingers had started to itch, sometimes, he had stopped me from scratching and other times he had stopped me picking at my face. And because also he'd filled my plate with food and told me to eat when I'd needed someone to do that. When I'd needed to be told when and what to eat. Take the butter, he'd say when I wouldn't have taken it. Take the honey and put it on your bread. And there was the sweetness of it. Of his butter and the honey from his bees. You wouldn't believe what eating that was like. And there was going to be a trial, and what was I supposed to say.

Sometimes, he flapped in through a window of the library or into my apartment and brushed right up against me. And when he did, when he touched me, I could feel the dryness and the looseness of his skin.

There was going to be a trial and I was a witness and really, the truth was that I had seen some things. Sometimes I thought maybe that I might be happy to talk about it. Maybe, I thought, I might be ready to say everything and everything about it. If only this time the police or the lawyers or whoever they were would really ask.

I was making soups and I was taking baths and showers, but the garden had a way of coming back like Lee did, just when I thought that he was gone. Just when I thought I was getting a handle on things, the garden would swoop down like a bird and pick at me with its long beak. It had a way of showing up and unraveling what I had stitched together. I could feel it pulling at the edges of things and it was getting harder to keep it all straight.

There was the little dragon Lee, with his ashy scales and his worried face. The Lee who had kept me company and given me some good advice. But there was too the man in the garden. The big man with the long arms and the eyes who could see us even in the dark. The man who one night found the apple pieces we'd been hiding in our beds. The man who we'd said sorry, sorry, sorry to for doing it, for picking the apples and for eating them, the man for whom that hadn't been enough. There would be both of them, the two of them, the each and every of them at the trial. Lee and that other Lee and those blue eyes too, watching us girls, listening to every word we said.

Girls' Choir

in the garden (too full of apples)

The garden was trickling right into us, and it was all long afternoons and dragging light. Summer was winding down and the apples were heavy down inside us. We were like ships laden now and so low in the water all rounded sails just billowing in even just the lightest breeze and we whispered all the time together and thought that maybe we would live forever sleeping in the tall grass.

We didn't talk much anymore and we grew slow and ox-eyed in the heat. We only moved sedately through the garden, climbing ladders and turning the heavy apples on their branches towards the light. We were so tired, when the bees came and buzzed around us, we let them linger. We didn't have the energy to wave them away.

The ladders began to creak underneath us as we climbed them, then Eleni put her foot on a rung one morning and it cracked. After that, we didn't touch the ladders and we left the trees. We only went down by the river and slept. After breakfast, Hercules would meet us by the pool and we would walk to the river and then we would lie down all together and spend the day asleep, our hands all tangled up in his warm and dusty fur.

We stopped going to Lee's table when he called us. When it was morning it was too hard to get out of bed and in the afternoons we would be nestled too far down into the grass to stir. The days tipped and all the hours rolled just right together. We would sleep and Lee would cook and we would come and eat when we felt like eating. Roasts at midnight sometimes, or fried brioche, our plates spilling over with the moonlight streaming into every corner of the room.

Hesper whispered that she wanted it to be like this forever. This stillness, this heaviness, this pause. One night though we were sleeping down by the river all in a pile, when we heard Hercules growling low down in his throat. And there was something, some wrongness, that twitched us suddenly awake. That snapped us to our feet and sent our blood pouring all through our veins like ice. Hercules crouched down in the grass and bent his head bristling and snapped his teeth. And we cried out and backed towards the river, but then a flashlight clicked on and there was a laugh and it was only Lee. Only smiling and saying, what's all this?

Hercules stood between us, switching his long tail back and forth and showing his teeth, but Lee only pulled a bone out of his pocket and handed it to him and said, come on now girls, it's time to come inside. And we brushed past the dog and left him and we followed Lee. The night was colder than we'd realized and we shivered in the darkness and we were glad for Lee and for the bright path his flashlight cut through the deep shadows of the trees.

Before we got inside though, Eleni turned and called to Hercules. Come on you old dog, she said. It's too cold out here for you. Just as she was calling though, just as she was saying Hercules, Lee reached around behind her and pulled her roughly in, right inside the house. And inside, in the sudden brightness of the kitchen, we saw that he had golden smudges on his fingers and on the backs of his hands. And he told us he'd gone into our rooms and changed the sheets. And he said he'd found all the apple pieces we'd been hiding there, the chewed bits of them that we'd been saving and the apples that we'd picked and hadn't eaten yet. He said he'd wondered where we'd got our bellies, and he said he should have known that we were stealing from the trees. And then he pushed us down onto the kitchen floor and said we'd gotten fat.

He said that girls like us were liars, that girls like us didn't deserve all the things he'd done for us. The meals he'd cooked us, the things he'd said, the way he'd worked so hard to get us well. And this is how he was repaid? he asked us, the smudges from the apples glowing golden on his hands. And one of us had gotten very quiet and one of us had hit her shoulder on the corner of the table when he'd pushed us and one of us was laid out flat right on her back and couldn't catch her breath.

And he was getting quite close down to one of us, pressing us down against the floorboards. She's bleeding. Look, she's bleeding, one of us said and that one of us was right because painted right along the floor there was a red wash of blood. Another one of us said, we're sorry, we didn't mean it. And another one of us whispered that we'd do anything to make it right.

But he only brought his face down low until it was almost touching us, until we could smell the hot air hissing out from in between his teeth and he was spitting then right on us when he shouted that he had told us that we shouldn't pick them. And look at you, just look at you, he said. And he gave us then a moment to feel the way we were disgusting, to have lied, to have picked the apples, to be girls with bodies that showed just openly everything we ate. To be fat. To have eaten as many of them as we wanted, as many of them as we did.

He reached into his pocket and then he grabbed our cheeks and started pressing the bits of skin and stem and core that he'd found hidden in our bedsheets down right into our mouth. And we were gasping then, and we were choking on the apples. And one of us put up our hands to try to block him and one of us tried to close her mouth but he only shoved more and more of them right down between our teeth.

Stop, we tried to say. But there were all those apples. And we were choking and they were foaming then right up behind our lips. All the apples and all the other things we'd ever lied about. Inside us it was all acid and bits of acrid pulp, all apple skin and apple stems and golden seeds and sick. And there were the apples, the gold of them, just tearing up our throats. We were sorry. We were so sorry we'd ever done it, but still there were his thumbs pressing down right into us.

One of us gasped, stop it. Please stop it, one of us said. And one of us said, she's not breathing and there was a coldness running then just all between us, all dark and limp and long and quiet, and that was when Hercules burst into the house.

In the end, he had come when Eleni called him. When she put her hand against the kitchen door and turned and said, come on you old dog, come in the house. We thought of him hearing her and we thought of how hard it was for him sometimes to pull himself up on his big feet. We thought of how we loved him and how we'd felt brave then or maybe powerful or golden, or even only just a little casual, when we'd acted then just for a moment like we'd owned that house. Like it was our garden, our apples, our home to invite him into. And we'd turned and said, come on you old dog, come in quick. We thought of how we'd been laughing then and passing through the door that Lee was holding open for us. Poor old dog, we'd said, calling him and rubbing the sleep out of our eyes and not seeing the smudges of gold just glistening here and there, smeared across Lee's skin.

Lee was terrible. He was so angry at us already, and when he was angry, he could be so strong. He heard poor Hercules behind him, and he tore around from us and grabbed him by his furry throat. And Hercules was all just popping eyes and lolling tongue and Lee was squeezing him so hard. And we were aching with all the apples down inside us and we couldn't ask Lee anymore to stop.

Lee lifted Hercules right off the ground until his legs were swinging and said, I told you not to come into the garden. He shook Hercules at us and said, this dog was always after my apples. Was always running through the garden and barking at the trees. Did you start stealing them for him? Is that it? Lee said. And we only just curled tight into little fists right where we were down on the floor. And we pressed our cheeks into the cool floorboards and we didn't look at Hercules and we only just said nothing and not that Lee had got it wrong, that our stealing apples had never been the poor dog's fault.

We got all small and quiet and we waited to see if any one of us would tell the truth, but we were so scared and we were so quiet and we never did. And then we made it worse for Hercules because one of us propped herself up on her bruised elbows and said that Lee was right, that it had all been Hercules's fault. That there were only apples in our sheets because Hercules had been coming and eating them there in bed with us at night. And the other ones of us nodded, our hot cheeks rocking wetly there against the floor. And we didn't tell Lee that nothing that had happened had been about the dog. Girls like us are liars, and we all were liars then, lying all together in the kitchen on the ground.

Then Lee carried Hercules outside like he weighed nothing, that huge dog who'd come and licked our ankles when we'd been high up on the ladders in the trees. And

Lee's arms were so long and Lee's hands were clamped like talons right around his throat. And we were breathing fine again and clearly. And we were so glad and so relieved to be released. We said again that the dog had made us do it. That it had been Hercules just all along. If it hadn't been for Hercules, we would never have done it, we said.

PART IV

(apples, liars, girls)

fourteen hours before the trial

Ari, Hesper, Eleni

The prosecutor was late, but we told him it was fine. Sitting all together in the hotel lobby tucked up in the plastic lobby chairs, we blinked at him when he arrived and told him it was not a problem. We were just catching up, we said. And we had been, we had been catching up and we had been eating apples. Just the green ones that sat out in the lobby baskets, gleaming all in waxy piles. The soggy, mealy kind that taste like wet sawdust when you take a bite.

And it had been so funny that we were there, in the lobby of the Marin Lodge Hotel, back together just like old friends. Just checking in with the boy at the reception desk, all just sunglasses and overnight bags and thanks-for-the-keys. And on top of everything, there were those apples in the lobby while we waited. And there we were, just eating them. Like oh, we do this all the time, sitting together eating apples, taking only the littlest little bites.

When we saw each other waiting in the lobby, we were not surprised. We said though to each other that we had been surprised to receive the letters. Who would have thought! we said. Who would have thought there would actually have been lawyers and a trial and involvement from the state!

It had been so long since we had seen each other. And there was a hitch down deep inside us, seeing each other so tangible and all at once, like dipping a finger into a fast-moving stream. We felt the pull of each other, we were heady with it, we fidgeted in our seats. Anyway seeing each other in the lobby, we could feel it. The way that we were tumbling somewhere together, getting swept off, rubbing up against an awful little pulse.

One of us had longer hair and one of us had painted nails and one of us looked sick. You look sick, we wanted to say, rolling the hotel apples around in our palms. And we wanted to touch each other and we didn't quite know how. And we wanted to ask each other how we had been. And we wanted to rest our cheeks right on each other's shoulders and ask, how had we been doing it this whole year just all alone?

And then the hotel lobby clock ticked over to five o'clock and the boy behind the reception desk clapped his hands together. Well that's it, it's happy hour ladies, he said. And he put two bottles of wine out on the lobby counter next to a stack of plastic cups. He told us that we could serve ourselves and he winked at us and told us that it was on the house. We said thanks and filled up the little complimentary cups.

So when the prosecutor came, we had been drinking. Not so very much, but enough that we were sitting back a little heavy in our chairs. Enough that we were leaning a little closer to each other, wanting to touch each other and to pull each other's different hair. The prosecutor was a very surprisingly young man with a blotch of mustard on his tie. He sat down at one of the tables in the lobby and motioned us over and he clicked open his briefcase and pulled out a pen and clicked that too against his teeth.

And we looked at him sitting at the table, at his mussed-up hair and at his tie. At his pants riding up and showing slouching purple socks and we thought, you? You're the one that's come? But we didn't say the things that we were thinking. Instead, we were quiet. All folded hands and crossed ankles and polite. We sat down with him at the table, giving the sicker one of us a moment to settle, to shift her bones delicately against the hard plastic of the seat.

This shouldn't take long, the prosecutor said when we were seated, I just wanted to get a few things straight. We don't usually have witnesses come out the night before but I wanted to go over the details so we can be clear on what's important before I get you up on the stand. And anyway, the Animal Defense League agreed right away to put you up when I asked them about the hotel. That's why we decided to do it this way, just so you know, he said.

We weren't sure if we were supposed to tell him thanks, or if we were supposed to tell him that it was not a problem, so we just nodded and sipped our drinks. Then he pulled out several yellow legal pads and a stack of printed papers and he spread these out on the table in messy stacks. He squinted at them, so we squinted at them too. All those notes and notes and notes. We tried to see where he might have written garden, or apple, or girl. We leaned down closer and closer to the table looking, trying to find where we might be hiding in all those notes. The prosecutor coughed and clicked his pen. Anyway, he said, frowning at us now, looking at us maybe with concern. Anyway, he said, let's get to it. And we said, yes absolutely let's. And we put our cups down on the table and we held hands. And we thought, this is it.

You were all at Mr Lotan's house the night of August the twenty-second of last year? he said. And we all nodded and said that was correct. OK great, the young prosecutor said, clicking his pen and writing. Perfect, he said. That's good. Really, just you being at Mr Lotan's house gets us most of the way there.

Oh good, we said nodding. Oh, excellent. Yes, the prosecutor said. It's really very simple. Mostly, I just need you to tell the court that you were there. And we thought, oh. And we let go of each other's hands and the sicker one of us pulled a small box of Fruit Loops from her pocket and peeled off the top. And she crinkled open the plastic bag on the inside and started eating the cereal one piece at a time, crunching each O loudly between her front teeth.

Seeing us sitting there at the table all together, or perhaps it was seeing us opening the cereal box, the teenager behind the front desk came over to tell us that usually there were crackers. Usually I put out crackers, he said, with the wine. Two kinds, he said, usually. Then he waited beside our table, pulling at the sleeves of his uniform and picking at something in his pocket until we told him thank you. It was fine, we said. We told him it was not a problem about the crackers. The prosecutor waved him away.

This conversation is private, the prosecutor told the teenager without looking up. State business, the prosecutor said. The teenager returned to the front desk. And did you see Mr Lotan shoot the dog? The prosecutor said, writing something on one of the papers. And we all nodded and said that we had. Good, he said. That's the main thing. Tomorrow, I'm probably just going to need you to say that you were there at Mr Lotan's house on the night in question and that you saw him shoot the dog. That's basically it, he said. We nodded and listened to him click his pen. But while you're here, I wanted to check on a few other details. Just so I'm clear regarding the situation, the prosecutor said.

We said that was fine. We said that was not a problem. The sicker one of us was licking her fingers and crinkling up the plastic bag. We had been getting hungry, but now we were feeling better. We were feeling then all sugar-rushed and flushed with wine and full and ready for the questions we'd been waiting for. Ask us, really ask us, we thought.

The police reports say they found the dog hanging up in a tree, the prosecutor said, reading through his papers.

Did you see Mr Lotan do that? Hang the dog? And we all nodded and said that we had. I'm not sure I'll want to complicate things, the prosecutor said. But just so I'm aware, did he shoot the dog and then hang it? Or was it the other way around? The autopsy was inconclusive, he said, on that point.

And there we hesitated. And we found we didn't want to remember. And we shifted in the lobby chairs that were suddenly much harder all against us and we bit our lips and sipped our drinks. Then the sicker one of us said, the other way around. And at the same time, another one of us said, yes. And the prosecutor clicked his pen and said, well which one is it? And we said we weren't sure.

The prosecutor sighed and said, OK, let's take it slowly. Let's take our time and figure this out. Because tomorrow you're going to have to be clear when you answer a question. You're going to have to have the details straight. So how about you just tell me what you remember, we can start with that.

And the sicker one of us stopped licking her fingers and instead she touched her neck. And we were going to say that really, we'd rather not get into it. That maybe calling us as witnesses had been a bad idea. That maybe there had been some kind of mistake. And we were pushing back against it and we were getting up to leave but then we did remember, and it was like snapping fingers and then it was too late. It was all fresh again and right in front of us just all laid out.

Hercules, his big head lolling on the kitchen floor and Lee standing over him, his hands around the poor dog's throat. That pink tongue hanging all wet and dragging and those huge, soft paws twitching on the kitchen floor. We remembered how Hercules had just been lying there. Just letting Lee tie him up. Don't just lie there, we tried to tell him. But we were too scared, too full of apples and too relieved to find Lee busy, his fingers lifted from around our throats.

We told the prosecutor Lee shot Hercules once he was up in the tree. Once he was already hanging. We remembered it now, how it happened, we said. Lee had choked Hercules, then Lee had tied him up and then Lee had hung him from the tree in front of the house. Then Lee had shot him and then the branch had cracked, and the dog had fallen down right underneath it. It happened just like that, we said.

And we could see then right in front of us, the way the branches of the apple tree were creaking, too heavy already with the weight of all that September fruit. And we saw Lee hauling Hercules out the front door. And we saw the limping way we followed, trailing after them. Not to help Hercules. Just to watch. Just to make sure it was Hercules Lee hated and not us. And for a moment we remembered the way the dog had rested his big head against Lee's shoulder while Lee was carrying him outside. But we pinched the insides of our arms and we told ourselves, stop, don't remember that.

We don't need to know that about the branch, the prosecutor said. I won't ask you that tomorrow. And the sicker one of us said he wasn't dead. The dog wasn't, she said, before Mr Lotan pulled him up into the tree. He was just choked. Just dazed, she said. Just out of breath.

That's fine, the prosecutor said. Don't worry, I'm not planning on asking you about that. We're just going to stick to the most important details. We don't want to risk you getting sidetracked in court. Really, I just need you to say that you saw Mr Lotan shoot the dog. Honestly, he said, this is a simple case. If, for example, I ask you if you saw Mr Lotan pull the dog up into the tree, I'm just going to need you to say yes. Don't get started in on telling me about the kind of tree it was. Don't go into apples or anything like that. And we leaned back in our chairs and crinkled up our plastic cups and said that we understood.

Well, that's pretty much it, the prosecutor said. I'm just going to quickly go over some background information with you. Just for my records, since I've got you here. Best to be thorough, he said. We asked him what he wanted to know.

The police report says that you were all living at Mr Lotan's house at the time, the prosecutor said, reading from his notes. And we nodded and we told him that was right.

Some kind of treatment facility, was it? the prosecutor asked us, his eyes flicking up and over us like he was dusting us for crumbs. Some kind of center? he said, reading from his notes. Golden Apples? he said. That the name of it? Of Mr Lotan's place? We all nodded, and we told him he was right.

It seems that you had all been living there for quite some time? the prosecutor said, still reading. And we nodded and we said yes. Quite some time, we said.

And you all left Mr Lotan's house the night of the twenty-second, after he shot the dog? And we all nodded. And you didn't go back to live there, after that? We said that was correct. We said he had it right. We said we did not go back after the night of the twenty-second, after he shot the dog. We did go back to get our things, the sicker one of us said, but we didn't go back after that. Right, we said. That was right, not after that.

And it was the neighbor who called the police? the prosecutor said, writing something down on his yellow pad. We told him yes, that it was the neighbor who called the police.

So you saw her that night? the prosecutor asked. The neighbor? And we told him that we had seen her. We said that the neighbor, hearing the gunshot and finding her dog missing, had come running to Lee's house. We said that we had seen her clearly. We said we saw her running in her slippers, in between the trees.

The prosecutor told us just to say that we had seen her clearly if he asked us. Keep it simple, he said. You don't need to say that about the slippers or the trees. We nodded and we told him that we understood. We promised that tomorrow at the trial, if he asked us, we would say that we had seen the neighbor clearly. We said that we would leave it at that.

And we had seen her clearly, the night of the twenty-second. She had been wearing her nightgown and had looked silly running. Silly and also not silly, owing to her face. We didn't say about the nightgown because the prosecutor didn't ask us what she'd been wearing when we'd seen her. Or what her face had looked like. We sensed that these were not important points.

And we didn't tell the prosecutor about the way the neighbor's face fell either, when she saw her dog lying underneath the broken branch. Or about the way she'd scrambled down on the ground to pull him out from under it, or about the way she'd looked up at the four of us. We didn't say that she'd looked silly and not silly and we didn't say that we suspected it was a common thing, to look silly and not silly, when you're ripped all open wide like that.

We kept it simple. We pressed our lips together as tightly as our knees. We tried to answer only just the questions he was asking. We picked and combed through the details and tried our best to find the important bits. We said that the neighbor had had her phone stuffed down into her pajama pocket. That it had bounced out when she'd come running down the drive and that she'd had to bend over and scrabble in the dirt to get it back. And we saw her whole soft belly spreading out and jiggling when she was bending down! the sicker one of us wanted to tell the prosecutor. Because of the way her pajama shirt sagged so low and open at the neck! But we shushed her. We told her not to say that about the neighbor's belly. We told the sicker one of us that that was not an important part. We told the prosecutor that the neighbor was crying when she called the police, and that the phone got dirt all over her face. But the prosecutor said he wouldn't ask us about that. Let's not get distracted, he said.

Just stick to the bits about the dog, the prosecutor told us. Just the bits where you saw Mr Lotan shoot it. The parts where you saw him up close. Maybe if I ask you, you can say you saw the neighbor call the police. That's really all we need to hear from you in court though, the prosecutor said. We'll keep it at that.

You did say that you had a good view? the prosecutor asked us. Of Mr Lotan and the dog? And we told him yes. We had a very clear view, we said. We told him that it had all happened right in front of us.

We didn't say that the dog's long nails had scraped the glass of the front window while Lee had hauled him up into the tree. We sensed that this was not an important point. We didn't say either that Hercules had always been quite a dirty dog and that he had left a greasy stain on the window where he'd been dragged along it. We didn't say the part about him lying in the grass right at our feet while Lee threw the rope up in the branches, and we didn't tell the prosecutor how we didn't bend down to scratch his ears or untie him or even loosen the rope. We had a very clear view, was what we said.

And had you known this dog? the prosecutor asked us. We told him that we had. We said that Hercules had often come into the garden and we said that Mr Lotan had yelled at the neighbor many times about this.

Was this dog aggressive? asked the prosecutor. Can you think of a reason Mr Lotan might have felt threatened when the dog came into the house?

We said no, the dog was not aggressive. We said that he drank water, sometimes if he was thirsty, right out of our hands. We said that he ran up and down alongside the pool barking when we were swimming in it sometimes in the afternoons. When we were letting the silky green algae brush against us in swirling clouds of the brightest emerald greens. The prosecutor wrote down something on one of his papers. Wrote possibly, drank water out of hands. Or barked at algae or wrote possibly down something else. So would you say that the attack was unprovoked? the prosecutor asked.

We said that we would say that. And we wondered if we were lying and we told each other it didn't feel like we were telling the truth. Shh, we said, don't say that. Not in front of the prosecutor. Keep it simple, we said.

And this was what? the prosecutor asked us, reading through his notes. About one o'clock in the morning? When Mr Lotan shot the dog? And we said yes, that must be about right. And we pinched each other and we told ourselves to be precise and helpful. And we sat up straighter in our chairs and sipped our drinks. Yes, yes, we said nodding, keeping it simple. One o'clock.

What were you all doing out there at one o'clock in the morning? he asked us after a moment. I'm not going to ask you that tomorrow. I don't want to distract from the dog. But still, it seems a bit odd, he said. The one o'clock thing. You all being up with Mr Lotan and the dog coming in the house. Was it some kind of therapy thing you were doing? he said. It's just that the defense attorney might ask. That is, if he decides to cross-examine you. I don't really expect him to, but anyway it's better if I know the answer to these sorts of things ahead of time.

We hesitated and we knocked our knees together underneath the table and we reached for our drinks and found we all had empty cups. Yes, we said. Sometimes we had things to do at night there. Things related to our treatment, the sicker one of us said looking at the prosecutor like she was daring him to ask. He didn't ask though and we settled back down in our seats while the prosecutor wrote possibly, related to treatment, next to the note marked one o'clock. And the dog must have heard you in the kitchen, the prosecutor said, reading. And come in. And we said yes, the dog must have heard us in the kitchen that night.

And was that unusual? the prosecutor asked us. And one of us said yes it was and another one of us said, no it wasn't. And we started to say that it was not unusual for us to be up in the middle of the night, but that that night had been quite different from other nights. The prosecutor stopped us though. No, he said, I meant about the dog. I meant was it unusual for the dog to come in the house like that.

We looked at each other and said it was, that it was quite unusual for the dog to come in. OK, said the prosecutor, writing something down. Writing perhaps, unusual or quite. Well, he said, anyway I seriously doubt the one o'clock in the morning business will come up. But if the defense asks, just say that it was usual for you to be awake. Or tell him that it was related to your treatment if you like. We told him we could do that. Not a problem, we said.

Well, said the prosecutor, that's about it. Just to make sure I'm not missing anything though, perhaps you could describe that night for me generally? He shuffled through his papers, frowning then he asked us, does anything come to mind?

And we held hands and we told each other; this is it. Now is when we talk if we're ever going to, we said. And it was like we were diving all together right into freezing water and the hotel lobby air snapped against us all suddenly like ice. And we took in a deep breath and said, the afternoon of the twenty-second Mr Lotan had cooked us duck. We said it clearly, like we were making an official statement. We said that he cooked it the way he did when he turned the heat way up high right at the end and threw cherries in the pan. We said how the cherries had hissed because they had just been washed and were dripping still with water. And sherry too, we said. He added sherry too, we told the prosecutor, and made a sauce. And we said that he had us eat it, the duck and the hot cherries, while he watched.

But the prosecutor sighed and pushed the hair back off his forehead and told us to stop. I mean, describe for me generally what you heard, or what you saw, in relation to the dog, he said. You have to remember why we're here. It's important not to get distracted. It's important to keep the focus where it should be in these sorts of things. Let's not forget, he said, a dog died that night.

We said yes, of course, and we promised that we would focus on only just the most important things. We apologized for bringing up the duck. We pinched each other and we chewed on the insides of our lips and cheeks and one of us had tears just starting at the corners of her eyes and one of us could feel a dampness on her back where there was sweat. That had been the wrong way to go about it, we said. We were sorry for the dog and he had died that night and we hadn't helped. The old, quite-dirty dog that we had really liked so very much.

We skipped the part where Lee, after cooking the duck had sent us out to tend the apples. And how, while we'd been out there, we'd fallen asleep and Lee had gone and changed our sheets. And we skipped the part about our shoulders pressing down against the kitchen floor and the part about the apples in our mouths, the kicking our feet against the table legs and the way we had arched our backs. And we skipped all the other things that we might have said. Shh, it won't come out right. We'll make a mistake if we try to tell it, we told ourselves. We'll talk about the cherries maybe. It's all too complicated, we said.

We skipped the part too about how Mr Lotan had been quite unhappy with us. And we skipped the part about the veins at the corner of Mr Lotan's forehead popping, and the part about how heavy his hands were all against us when he pushed us down. We didn't talk about how he'd pulled a handful of rustling, golden cores out of his pockets and hissed at us that he could see that we were the types of girls who went behind his back. The type of selfish, greedy girls who ate too much. He could see that we were like that, everyone could see it, he had told us. And we didn't want the prosecutor to write greedy down in his notebook. We told each other we didn't want that.

The dog trusted Mr Lotan, we added. Even though Mr Lotan was sometimes rough with him. Even though sometimes Mr Lotan yelled at him, we said. The dog had maybe loved him a little, we said.

We skipped so many parts. We're skipping everything! one of us said. And we told that one of us to just be quiet, and we told that one of us that maybe skipping things was for the best. Just watch how we can soar right over all the messy bits! we said. We thought that maybe we could fly right over all of it tomorrow too when we were at the trial, like the way pelicans skim low over ocean swells and don't get wet. We thought maybe we wouldn't ever have to say the way that Lee had been so angry with us, or how he pushed us and called us greedy and called us fat. We don't have to say about how we ate those apples, we told each other. We don't have to say about how we ate them and ate them and couldn't stop. And we felt relief shiver through us, thinking how we wouldn't have to tell anyone after all about the way we didn't help the dog, about how we'd let him down when he had needed us.

Don't say that about the dog maybe loving Mr Lotan, the prosecutor said. I don't need you speculating, it's not useful on the stand. And we made our eyes wide and round and we nodded attentively like we were taking notes. Absolutely, we won't mention it, we said.

Good, the prosecutor said. Good to know we're all on the same page. So, to sum up, tomorrow you'll say at the trial that on the night of August the twenty-second Mr Lotan shot the dog. Does that sound doable? the prosecutor asked us. And we said yes, it absolutely did. Then he asked us if we had any questions. And one of us wanted to know if we should say the part about the apples. Or about the tree and the branch and the tying up? And one of us wondered if we should say that Hercules had liked the apples. To give a picture, that one of us said, of what he was like?

I wouldn't think so, the prosecutor said. We don't want to make it sound as if the dog was stealing. We need to underscore that this was unprovoked. We said we could skip the part about the apples. That's probably for the best, the prosecutor said.

One of us thought maybe we should start again. Maybe we should try to explain it differently, that one of us said. But the prosecutor said he thought he had a pretty good idea of the situation. One of us was thinking that maybe if we only hadn't started with the cherries and the duck. Maybe he would want to hear more of what we had to say, that one of us was wondering, if only we could say it better, if only we could get it right. We told her we wouldn't get it right. We'll talk about the cherries again, we told her. Or if not the cherries, then the duck. It was good duck though, she said. And we said yes, it had been very good duck.

So we promised to keep it simple and the prosecutor told us that was good. Just answer the questions that I ask you tomorrow when I have you on the stand and stick to the important bits. We told him that we'd stick to the point. We told him we understood that the dog was the point.

Right, said the prosecutor. Just remember that tomorrow and we'll get this guy. Jesus, he said, shooting a dog like that. Can you imagine? It's just so awful, the prosecutor said. The neighbor lady, she hasn't gotten over it. I've met with her a couple of times in my office. She's in a terrible state. These cases, just between you and me, they're the worst. Anyway, he said, picking up his papers and putting them back in his briefcase, that's about all I need.

After he had gone, we went to our rooms. Three singles, each with a window facing the parking lot. We ended up all together in the middle room, lying on the bed just like sardines. We pushed against each other and for a while it was all hair catching and hard elbows and one of our knees in another one's back.

The conversation with the prosecutor had been like that. We thought that really, it had been exactly like a knee in the back. Which is to say it had been mostly fine, mostly not a problem, but something that made you lie down very still throughout. We were thinking though that the conversation with the prosecutor had missed some things.

But how do we know it's not better this way? we said. Another one of us said we shouldn't have started with the duck. We should have started with something more important. Something he would listen to. But the duck was important, we said.

And then we looked up at the clock and we said, look, it's ten hours before the trial. And Eleni said, let's not wait that long to see Lee. And we laughed and we said what was she talking about, but she was already pulling us up off the bed.

seven hours and twenty-five minutes before the trial

Ari

It had been so long since I'd seen those eggs. Since I'd smelled the hot, fried-brown butter of them or seen the way the salt rested lightly on those wet, golden yolks. Eleni had already finished the grapes that Lee had made her and she was all soft now and her eyes were closed and there was color in her cheeks. Hesper was leaning down into her potatoes, breathing in the steam of them and flipping them over with her fork. The girl in the white dress though was already eating, already shoveling the gleaming carrots in her mouth.

Lee said that it was nice to see us, that he had thought we might be visiting tonight. And his voice was just so light and friendly and fell so softly on us sitting in our chairs and he was putting his hands on our shoulders and saying really, it had been too long. And it had been too long, we thought then. Remembering what it had been like sometimes at his table. Remembering how in the mornings he would tell us we were looking well, remembering how he'd smiled sometimes cooking at the stove, flipping pancakes, making jokes.

He'd missed us, he said. And we felt so warm then and we remembered just what it had been like when he had loved us. When he'd thought that we were special girls and told us we were precious to the world. We remembered how it was before he found the apples, when we would sit all at his table and eat food that was not like anything we had ever tasted before. When we were getting better and getting fixed. Tell us that we're good, we wanted to say, seeing him like that in his kitchen after it had been so long.

The carrots were almost gone. Even though she'd started with such an enormous heap. We watched while she shoved the last of them into her mouth, the glaze all running freely down her chin. And Lee smiled down at her and picked up a napkin and began to dab at the drips. Look at you, he said. Getting butter everywhere like that. The girl didn't seem to feel him wiping though. She didn't react. She only let him touch her, only let him slide the napkin down her neck. And we wondered if he'd ever dabbed our chins that way without us knowing it. We wondered if he'd ever touched us with a napkin like that.

We were wondering but also we were eating. Hesper had a whole potato in her mouth and I had split the yolks with the edge of my fork. There was the salt and the crisp edges and the glistening fat and when I finally took a bite, it was everything that I remembered and everything that I'd forgot.

Then our plates were clean and we were suddenly much more than tired. And we thought, what if we woke up tomorrow morning to Lee's fresh bread and blackberry jam. What if we knew that we would eat it? We thought about the butter that we would spread so thickly on it and the ripe apricots we might eat with it or the dates. What if we should stay? we thought and polish another year's worth of apples. What if it was safer here than anywhere else?

One of us said, haven't we been hungry? And another one of us said yes. And we wondered if really, we might be taking better care of ourselves if we were to stay. Who can say, we said, if this isn't what we need? And one of us thought oh, it's June. And we thought of the corn cakes Lee had made the year before all studded through with summer nectarines. How we'd eaten them by the pool in the cool evenings with boysenberries and poured cream. And we thought oh, how could we miss all that? For what? For doctor appointments? And to be told about tuna sandwiches? And two tablespoons of almond butter? we thought.

We thought maybe we'd been wrong about a lot of things. And we thought about how so many times Lee had been right. We asked ourselves if we'd been silly. What had we been scared of walking down the drive? We thought that maybe we'd just forgotten. That maybe we'd remembered wrong all this time.

And we really were so tired. And we thought that really, we should go upstairs. And we picked up our clean plates and put them in the sink. But then there was the tap of something hitting the floor and we saw Eleni's hands had come uncurled down in her lap and that she'd dropped her bread. And we saw then that she was asleep, or that maybe she was more than just asleep because of how she was tipping in her seat and because of how her chin was rocking down to hit the trail of oil and wine and juice that spread so redly out across the front of her shirt.

We grabbed her and she was so heavy then against us and we saw that Lee had reached out to grab her too.

You should go on up to bed, he told us and we felt then how our heads were swimming. How there was a fuzziness to the edges of the things we saw. We rocked back on our heels and we wondered if we might be falling. Are we going to fall? we asked him but Lee just only told us to hand her over, to give her here. And really, she was so heavy for us and he had always been so strong, so quite easily able to hold us up.

We were going to give her to him. But it was only just that then she tipped her head against us, only just that then she rested her head against our shoulders and we remembered Hercules and how he'd tipped his head against

Lee's shoulder and that still Lee had taken him outside and strung him up. We knew then that we'd remembered right before, that we'd been right before when we'd been so afraid.

She slipped against us and between our arms, heaving and sliding slowly to the floor. Lee stepped towards us and told us we were tired. You're tired, you can't go anywhere with her like that, he said. Look at you, he said to Hesper, with that leg. And he was walking towards us with his arms outstretched and we were trapped again in that same cage and he was right, we couldn't hold Eleni up.

We felt the doors of that cage then closing right against us, pressing us towards our rooms, back up the stairs. And we could see how we might come down them in the morning, how the food would be delicious and how we might go on like that forever, polishing the apples every summer as they grew.

There was more though, more outside, more than the cage and the door of it closing. Can you feel that? we said and we said yes we could. It was the apples on the branches, all those golden apples twisting on their stems. We could feel them then just like we could feel each other. And we remembered all the things that had happened to us in this house. We could feel the gold of them running through us. Tendrils, stems, and roots. We said had it been like this all along?

Lee grabbed Eleni's wrist and pulled her to him. As soon as she was in his arms, we felt him holding her. This made us suddenly wrathful, suddenly wild and so hateful and we took in an enormous breath like we were drawing in a storm and brought the apples hard down on the roof. It was easy, it was a relief, bringing down the apples. All we had to do was reach for them and twist them off their stems just exactly like we were picking them with our own hands.

Lee was holding Eleni still but his face had fallen. He cringed a little at the pounding on the roof and we could feel the way that he was slowly pushing her away. There was sweat beading out and slipping down his forehead. He said, now girls, now girls, listen. But we only shook our heads.

There was a crash from up above us, girls yelling to each other about the roof. It's broken, it's coming down, we heard them saying. And we thought of all those apples raining down so hard on those little made-up beds. Three girls came running down the stairs then and right into the kitchen, crying and begging Lee to make it stop.

Eleni stood up straight all on her own and Lee slapped her hard across the face. He told us that what we were doing was sick, that we had to make it stop. But outside now it was more than apples. Outside now there were branches falling from the trees. And we smiled despite the spreading blue bruising Eleni's cheek as the orchard started coming down around the house. We smiled at the snapping twigs outside the windows and the crack of branches as they hit the roof. Can you feel it? we said. And we said that we could feel it. It feels good. It feels really good, we said.

Lee let Eleni go because he couldn't hold her. No one could hold us, we thought. Not like this, not with us so reckless and so full. And we thought about the trial and about the poor old dog, the way that he had licked and licked our ankles, and we brought the big old apple tree where he had hung crashing down through the front of the house.

We thought Look at this, all from eating apples! And we laughed and thought that really, all those apples we had eaten had made us very strong. We ran whooping right into the living room, laughing to feel the orchard tumbling outside as we went. All the trees that we had tended, all empty now of apples, we could feel them tipping and ploughing themselves freely right into the ground.

By the time we got into the living room to see it, the big broken tree lying in the gaping ruin of the house, we could see that out beyond it there was a kind of lightly gusting golden dust. Like pollen, falling down and dazzling and filling up the air. We held hands and watched it all the three of us together. The downed branches, the fallen trees and the wreckage of the house, all of us all caught now together in a swirling golden haze. And we thought that maybe this was what we'd come for. That maybe this whole year we'd been counting down just all the hours between us and this.

Then Lee came into the room and all the air ran out of it behind him and we shivered down inside ourselves and it was very cold. And we were small again and just ourselves and all emptied out of apples and one of us said run.

We leapt right through the broken window then, right into the fallen tree and two of us went tearing through the branches but one of us was quiet, lying there quite still and stuck. Then two of us were running through the ruined garden, but one of us was lying in the branches, still inside the house. How can we leave her? Hesper gasped then just behind me. But I was already opening the door of Lee's old van and yelling at her to get in. I pulled the spare keys out from the spot underneath the driver's seat where I knew Lee hid them and I turned the car on and switched on the lights.

There lit up in the headlights was Eleni and we watched while two girls in white dresses pulled her back inside the house. We hesitated even then with the car running. In the seat beside me Hesper asked how we could leave. But the van door slammed behind us and we turned to see the girl who'd been given the plate of honeyed carrots sitting in the back. Her eyes were dark as tunnels bored straight back into the paleness of her face and she said go, go, go, before he gets us. And then we were driving, reversing up the curving drive, swerving around the newly fallen trees.

In the headlights, we saw Lee chasing after us. We saw how he was almost flying, how he was running faster than it seemed possible to run. Behind him we saw Eleni with the other girls inside the house. We saw them hold her gently by the broken window and dab at her face with a little polishing cloth. Hesper said, oh how can we bear to leave her but I was wondering how we could ever bear to make her come. Inside the house, the other girls smoothed Eleni's hair and hugged her. Then we turned the corner and backed out onto the road and she was gone.

the trial

Ari

Driving down the road near the ocean, close enough that we could smell the salt, the sun was coming up and we could see the first golden rays of it breaking out into the blue. And I was thinking of the way Lee had tucked the hair behind my ears and told me I was precious. How he'd told us that we kept him young. How sometimes the lines around his blue eyes would crinkle up and how he would tell us that we were beautiful. I wondered if I had wanted the prosecutor to ask me whether there were things about the garden that I missed.

Did you ever say no to Mr Lotan? the prosecutor might have asked us if we'd been subpoenaed as witnesses to another sort of trial. And I would have had to say that I hadn't, that I'd never said anything to him but yes. So maybe it was better to keep it simple and let us be just only witnesses to this thing that had happened there to that poor dog.

And maybe we could anyway get only part way out of the garden once we'd been there or maybe there was no getting out once we'd gone back. We asked the girl in the back if she had somewhere to go, if there was somewhere we could take her. But she said no, so none of us had anywhere to be. We headed north, running down the tank in Lee's old van. We wondered if the apple trees would grow again or if they wouldn't. One of us thought that probably there would always be a garden out there by the ocean and one of us thought that there would probably always be girls there too. And another one of us thought that there always must be girls in gardens tending apples. Clipping branches and polishing the fruit, being golden and tending the new year's crop.

But we, we were driving. We though, we were slipping off our golden skin. There would be a trial and we might be there, or we might not be. There would be a young prosecutor waiting to ask us questions about a dog and we might or we might not be there to answer them. We were coming out from beneath our skins. We were driving, we were taking big breaths of all that clean ocean air.

We were still heading north when we came over a rise and the sun hit the windshield, washing us out for a moment in a burst of blinding light. Maybe someday Eleni would call us and tell us she'd left the garden and maybe she never would. And when we came over some other rise, the next one maybe, or some other farther one, some day down the road, we would be saying only just the usual things. Only, let's pull over here, or let's have lunch. We would be only as good as we wanted to be, only as pleasing as pleased us and none of what we were saying would be anything but small and light and true on our fresh skin, it would not be incomplete or covering over, and none of it would be a lie. It would not be.

KYRA WILDER grew up in the Pacific Northwest and went on to study at the Culinary Institute of America. She cooked in restaurants in New York and California and was the pasta maker in Michael Tusk's now Michelin-starred restaurant, Quince, before receiving her BA and MA in English Literature from San Francisco State University. She continued working in restaurants before moving to Switzerland with her young family and subsequently publishing her first novel, *Little Bandaged Days*. Her poetry and articles have been published in *The Paris Review*, *Literary Hub* and *McSweeney's*.

In 'the quick brown fox' collection:

Penelope Curtis
After Nora

Lauren Elkin
*No. 91/92: notes on
a Parisian commute*

Erica van Horn
We Still Have the Telephone

Michèle Roberts
French Cooking for One

Charlotte Beeston
The White Flower

Kyra Wilder
Gloss

In translation from French:

Catherine Axelrad
Célina
trans. Philip Terry

Jean Frémon
*Now, Now, Louison;
Nativity,* trans. Cole Swensen
Portrait Tales, trans. John Taylor

Mireille Gansel
Translation as Transhumance
trans. Ros Schwartz

Maylis de Kerangal
Eastbound
trans. Jessica Moore

Julia Kerninon
A Respectable Occupation
trans. Ruth Diver

Camille Laurens
Little Dancer Aged Fourteen
trans. Willard Wood

Noémi Lefebvre
*Blue Self-Portrait
Poetics of Work*
trans. Sophie Lewis

Nathalie Léger
Suite for Barbara Loden
trans. Natasha Lehrer
Exposition
trans. Amanda DeMarco
The White Dress
trans. Natasha Lehrer

Emilienne Malfatto
May the Tigris Grieve for You
trans. Lorna Scott Fox

Lucie Paye
Absence
trans. Natasha Lehrer

Shumona Sinha
Down with the Poor!
trans. Teresa Lavender Fagan

Clara Schulmann
Chicanes, trans. Clem Clement,
Ruth Diver, Lauren Elkin, et al.

Anne Serre
*The Governesses;
The Fool and Other Moral Tales*
trans. Mark Hutchinson

Sylvie Weil
Selfies
trans. Ros Schwartz